S

Hans Brunner is a dual citizen of Switzerland and Australia and lives near Zurich with his wife and three children. Formerly a press correspondent, he now works as controller for the international edition of *USA Today*. His many books for adults and children have been translated into eight languages and have won several literary awards.

Survivors!

Hans Brunner

Translated by Anthea Bell

Pan Piper

PAN MACMILLAN
CHILDREN'S BOOKS

First published in Great Britain 1989 by Macmillan Children's Books

This Pan Piper edition published 1992 by Pan Macmillan Children's Books
a division of Pan Macmillan Publishers Limited
Cavaye Place London SW10 9PG
and Basingstoke

Associated companies throughout the world

ISBN 0-330-32507-8

Copyright © 1987 Verlag AARE Solothurn [Translated by Anthea Bell]

The right of Hans Brunner to be identified as the
author of this work has been asserted by him in accordance
with the Copyright, Designs and Patents Act 1988.

1 3 5 7 9 8 6 4 2

A CIP catalogue record for this book is available from
the British Library

Printed in England by Clays Ltd, St Ives plc

1944

The three boys did not look like soldiers, although they were wearing German Army uniform.

Now and then one of them would glance furtively at the door. But nobody came in. The rain kept on beating against the small window. Its glass had misted over long ago. The room was overheated, and when the boys breathed out they produced little clouds of condensation. They had arrived three hours before. A sergeant had directed them to this small room, where they had been waiting ever since. The room smelled of chalk, floor polish and wet coats. Only a school classroom could smell like that. The smell, however, was all that was left of school in this particular room. The boys themselves had been at their classroom desks a year ago: only a year, but if asked how long it was, they would have had to stop and think. It was more than any of them could really grasp. They hadn't volunteered to join up. Somehow or other, school had simply stopped and boys became men. Reinforcements for the Front, now that Germany was crumbling on all sides. They had been at war for a year now. They were no heroes; they had been scared stiff right from the start. They were only boys who used to think war was an adventure, like something in the movies, and it turned out to be nothing but dirt, mud, blood and death. And waiting.

3

Waiting and more waiting. Waiting for the next order, the attack, the retreat, the next shell, the last bullet. The Eastern Front. Fifteen hundred kilometres away, three days and nights in a bumpy truck all the way across Germany and France, through ruins, bombed cities, chaos. The war was lost, even though it still ground on like a machine that wouldn't stop until it had destroyed itself.

'France,' said Hermann Karasek. 'Well, better than the Eastern Front, anyway.'

The two other lads nodded, agreeing. Hermann Karasek was the eldest of the three. Seventeen he had claimed to be, adding a few months on. He felt much older than Klaus Metzer and Paul Seidler, and he had a lance-corporal's stripe on his uniform.

'Do you think we'll get to meet Admiral Dönitz?' asked Paul.

Hermann laughed mockingly. 'You must be crazy! Admirals have other things to think about!'

'A colonel shook hands with me once,' said Paul. 'In the barracks, that was, when we'd done our training. The whole class was there. He said we were the nation's pride. And thanks to us it would all be over in a year.'

Klaus Metzer laughed without humour. 'Not a bad joke, that,' he muttered.

Hermann Karasek swung round. 'What did you say?'

'Nothing,' replied Klaus, undismayed. 'And it doesn't matter now, anyway. Got a cigarette?'

Paul handed him a crumpled cigarette packet and matches.

'Don't start on that again,' he said peaceably. 'We're all in the same boat, right?'

'Not Klaus and me,' replied Hermann Karasek.

4

'I've had about enough of his snide comments. You hear, Klaus? Any more remarks like that and I'll report you.'

Klaus Metzer shrugged his shoulders. 'Who to?' he inquired, scornfully. 'You don't even know where we're going.'

'Of course I know!'

'Because you've got a stripe? Come on, admit it. You've no more idea than we have.'

'I looked inside one of the crates,' retorted Hermann Karasek, triumphantly. 'That's how I know.'

'What crates?'

'The crates on the lorry. They were open.'

'What was in them, then?'

'Communications equipment. Radios and that. All new.'

'So?' said Klaus Metzer, unimpressed. 'We're in Communications, right?'

'That's just it: we're in the infantry. The stuff in those crates belongs to the Navy.'

'You sure?'

'Of course I'm sure! Would they have dragged us all the way here to Reims otherwise? I tell you, we're going on a ship!'

Klaus and Paul looked at one another, surprised.

'I've never been on a ship,' said Paul at last. 'Can't even swim.'

'I don't suppose that'll make any difference,' said Hermann Karasek. 'You didn't volunteer to join up in the first place, did you?'

Paul and Klaus shook their heads.

'They cancelled my leave,' grumbled Klaus. 'It was due in a fortnight. Hey, is it true that you have to be short to get posted to a ship?'

5

'What d'you mean?'

'Well, when the corporal gave me my marching papers he said: "For once you can be thankful you're only one metre fifty-five tall." '

'Size has nothing to do with it,' said Hermann Karasek, loftily. 'It's a person's mental attitude that matters. And yours is lousy.'

'Oh, shut up, will you?' said Klaus Metzer angrily. 'This war's as good as over – anyone can see that. The three of us aren't going to make any difference, are we? All I want to do is survive. When it's all over I'll go back to school, and then I want to forget about it as fast as I can.'

Before either of the others could say anything, the door opened and an officer came in. He stared at the three boys in surprise for a moment, and then pulled himself together.

'Hartmann,' he introduced himself. 'Lieutenant Hartmann. You can sit down . . . kids! My God, I didn't know we were in such a bad way as this. Oh, well. I suppose you know something about radio communications?'

'Yes, sir,' said the three boys, almost in chorus.

'Operation Frostbite,' said Lieutenant Hartmann. 'You're posted to U 98.'

'Going on a submarine?' asked Hermann Karasek incredulously.

Lieutenant Hartmann laughed. 'What did you expect? U 98 is the pack leader. Wolfpack Frostbite – three U-boats in all. We operate in the Indian Ocean. Around latitude sixty degrees south – know where that is?'

The three boys looked at each other, baffled.

'The Antarctic,' Lieutenant Hartmann told them. 'Down near the South Pole. It's our job to intercept

6

and destroy enemy convoys. Convoys of ships, understand? Freighters and tankers. Anything on its way to England. They're sailing farther and farther south to avoid our other U-boats in the Indian Ocean. There are four submarine packs operating already. We're going to close the last gap. Any questions?'

Hermann Karasek was the first to recover from his surprise. 'Why us?' he asked. 'We're not in the Navy.'

'Don't worry, we don't want to make sailors of you,' replied Lieutenant Hartmann. 'Your job's to operate a radio station so that Wolfpack Frostbite can keep in touch with her sister units.'

'Where's this radio station going to be?' asked Klaus Metzer.

'Right now the gear's being unloaded from the lorries and taken on board the U-boats. There are two more submarines sailing along with U 98. The final location of the radio station hasn't been decided yet. Maybe Kaiser Wilhelm II Land. It has to be a tactically good spot. Could be an island, too. Karpog, for instance. There'll be a depot for provisions and fuel as well as the radio station. We have enough supplies to keep Wolfpack Frostbite going for eighteen months.'

'Eighteen months!'

'That's right. I hope you've said your goodbyes.'

1979

1

On the Kingfish 1 oil production platform, Colin
Webster jammed the receiver close to his ear. Recep-
tion was bad, although the radio call came only from
the Australian mainland. He was talking to Jack
Morgan of Almax Shipping. The first part of their
conversation was in clear.

'Almax to Kingfish 1. Can you hear me, Kingfish
1?'

'Loud and clear, Almax. Come in.'

'Expect the tanker *Almax Venturer* for loading
on the twenty-fourth.'

'*Almax Venturer*'s already booked in for the twenty-
fourth, Almax. Five thousand tons of crude oil.
Loading time, about six hours. Docking time, twelve
noon. Confirmation?'

'Negative. Cancel the order. I repeat: the old
order's cancelled. New time of arrival, eight p.m.
Cargo to be taken on, fifty thousand tons.'

'What?'

'I repeat: fifty thousand tons.'

'But Jack . . .'

'Not in clear, Kingfish. Switch the chopper on.'

The chopper was a small device which scrambled
radio waves, converting them into an incomprehen-
sible electro-magnetic jumble. This jumble of sound

11

was all any eavesdropper could have heard. Only someone with another such device could receive the message in clear.

Colin Webster, on Kingfish 1, had one of these devices.

After a short break, the conversation went on.

'Are you crazy, Jack?' inquired Colin Webster. 'The Hastings refinery will never take fifty thousand tons from you.'

'The oil's not for Hastings, Colin.'

'But the *Almax Venturer*'s down for Hastings.'

'*Was* down for Hastings, Colin,' said Jack Morgan. 'Not any more. Like I told you, we've changed our plans.'

'Where, then?'

'What do you mean?'

'Come off it, Jack! Where's she going now?'

'To Helcheman, in Rotterdam.'

'You must be joking!'

'I never felt less like joking in my life, Colin. Almax Shipping needs that fifty thousand tons.'

'It won't pay you, Jack. The transport costs are too high. The Europeans can get their oil much cheaper from the Gulf states.'

'But not for long.'

'That's just rumour, Jack. The oil ministers have been meeting for over a week now, and they still haven't managed to agree on higher prices.'

'Prices are already rising, though, Colin.'

'They'll fall again just as fast once the conference is over and has proved inconclusive.'

'Maybe,' Jack admitted, 'but by then we'll have sold our cargo.'

Colin laughed disbelievingly. 'This idea's just a gamble, Jack! You're planning to start out with a tanker full of oil, hoping oil prices will rise during the voyage. By the time you reach Rotterdam, they could have fallen again just as quickly.'

'Oh, come on, Colin!' said Jack impatiently. 'We need this deal with Helcheman. They'll pay right away. I've been in business long enough to know we're taking a risk, but if we don't take it we'll go bust in two or three months' time.'

'As bad as that?'

'Worse. The *Almax Venturer* should have been in dry dock long ago. She's been due for inspection these last six months. Luckily the bureaucratic wheels turn slowly, or we'd have no ship and no money. As long as the *Almax Venturer* can put to sea there's at least some hope.'

'You know I can't sell you fifty thousand tons. Your credit's only good for seven and a half thousand.'

'Don't try that one on me, Colin! We're old friends. Surely you won't force me to do business with some other agent?'

Colin Webster laughed out loud. 'You can always try it, Jack.'

Both men knew that Almax Shipping had been on the verge of bankruptcy for over a year. No other agent would accept the risk, the delays in payment, the trouble with the banks. Colin Webster himself would have been glad to get rid of Almax's business. Only his old friendship with Jack Morgan kept him from doing just that.

'Fifty thousand tons is a huge cargo of oil, Jack. Can the *Almax Venturer* carry it?'

'She's registered for fifty thousand tons, Colin.'

'I know, but she's an old ship. When did she last carry fifty thousand?'

'Can't tell you that off the cuff.'

13

'I can, Jack. Never. Let's not kid ourselves. I've been your agent since you started with Almax, and I've never let you down yet, okay?'

'So I get the oil?'

Colin Webster hesitated for a moment. 'On one condition: I must have the *Almax Venturer* as security. And I want to see a copy of the entry in the shipping register before we start loading.'

'I don't know if I can fix it in time, Colin.'

'You will, Jack.'

'It'll be a close thing. If I'm lucky I can send the papers out with the tender.'

'A tender for the *Almax Venturer*? I thought you were short of cash.'

'I can't very well send her out without supplies, can I?'

'Where is she now?'

'On her way to you from Sydney. After that, she was going to the Hastings refinery, but now we've changed our plans they'll be needing additional water and supplies on board. I can't lose any time. Hence the tender.'

'Why didn't they take supplies aboard in Sydney?'

'Didn't know they were going to Rotterdam, did they?'

Colin Webster whistled softly through his teeth. 'When are you going to tell them?'

'Tomorrow morning. The captain knows. He'll speak to the crew in the morning. Before the tender arrives, I hope.'

'Your usual crew?'

'Yeah, same as always. Two new crew members, replacing Ed and Arthur. She was struck by lightning off the west coast. Ed and Arthur got hurt.'

'Badly?'

14

'No. Seems the lightning struck the foreship – had the *Almax Venturer* all lit up like something out of *Star Wars*. It took forever for the lightning to discharge. Did you ever see a ship struck by lightning? It runs along the metal parts like a welding flame. Ed and Arthur were standing by the rail aft. They both got burns on their hands.'

'You won't be very popular with the men – five weeks at sea, putting in only once on the way. They're not used to it, Jack. They've never done anything but potter along the coastline before.'

'They'll have the option. If they don't like the idea they can sign off.'

'Some option, Jack! With hundreds of applicants for every job, they'll think twice about that.'

'They're well paid. Better than they would be on shore, anyway. It's about time they did something for their money.'

Colin Webster laughed. 'I wouldn't like to be there when they hear the news,' he said. 'It'd have been grounds for mutiny in the old days.'

'Those days are long gone, Colin. Well, what about it? Do I get the oil?'

'Okay. In return for a copy of the entry in the shipping register certifying that the ship's my surety.'

'Don't trust an old friend much, do you?'

'Fifty thousand tons, unsecured, is too much to ask of any friendship. Even with the *Almax Venturer* as security I'm liable to have sleepless nights.'

Jack Morgan laughed drily. 'Feelings are just so many figures to you, Colin, don't kid yourself!'

'Well, we'll see. I'm coming on shore-leave in a couple of weeks, and about time too. We've had several nasty autumn storms, real brutes. I'll call you when I'm in Melbourne.'

15

'We could meet and have a meal somewhere.'

'I'll take you up on that invitation. Maybe we'd better make it a hamburger joint, what with Almax's financial difficulties.'

'They won't last much longer,' Jack Morgan assured him. 'As soon as we've done this deal with Helcheman business will start booming, Colin, you wait and see.'

Colin Webster muttered something inaudible under his breath. Then he asked, 'You're sure, are you, Jack? I mean, this isn't just some wild plan you've thought up hoping to save your bacon?'

'Don't worry, Colin. It's going to work out.'

Colin Webster gazed thoughtfully at the now silent loudspeaker. Jack Morgan's plan was a simple one . . . simple, but risky. As soon as the oil was in the ship's tanks, it belonged to Almax. If prices kept rising until the ship reached Rotterdam, then Almax would make several million dollars on the cargo. However, if prices suddenly dropped . . .

'Ah, what the hell?' said Colin Webster, out loud. 'Jack Morgan's weathered plenty of storms before.'

2

Monday, 9.30 hours

The regular waves of the swell rolled against the
bows of the *Almax Venturer*. The foreship rose and
fell with the rhythm of the sea, as if it had a life
of its own instead of belonging to the rest of the
two-hundred-and-fifty-metre tanker.

Anyone standing at the rail by the superstructure
in the stern could watch the movement of the waves:
first they raised the bows, sometimes by two metres or
more, then the foreship, and by the time they reached
the middle of the ship the bows had already dropped
back into the trough of the next wave.

When the ship was running straight into the swell
a slight shudder ran through her hull, and now and
then the twin propellers hummed aloud as they were
raised almost to the surface.

'Feeling bad again?' asked John MacGraw. There
was no sympathy in his voice, just the experience of
a man who had gone through it all long ago.

'Doesn't it ever get any better?' asked Peter Bush,
pushing strands of fair hair back from his face. He
was just fifteen, and this was his first voyage.

John MacGraw laughed soundlessly, his mouth
splitting his thick beard like a wide gash.

'I know seamen who were seasick from the day
they signed on till the last day the drew their pay.

17

No one knows why. Sometimes I feel that way myself, and not in a particularly high sea either.'

'I didn't really plan to sign on as a seaman,' said Peter. 'I once went to Tasmania on the ferry. It only took a day, and the sea was calm, but I felt sick to my stomach the whole way. I shouldn't have listened to Uncle Ben.'

'Ben Lexon, right? He got you the job,' said John MacGraw.

'How do you know?' asked Peter.

'Oh, it's no secret,' replied John MacGraw. 'Ben Lexon's a big shot in the union. There's no harm in pulling a few strings, son. Don't let it bother you if the others talk. They'd do just the same if they had the chance.'

'You too?'

'Me too,' smiled John MacGraw.

'I guess he really was being helpful,' said Peter, thoughtfully. 'Not that I asked him to. I needed a break, you see. I'd had enough of school. I might go back and study later, but I wanted to do something different first.'

'Well, you've got that here all right.'

'So Uncle Ben fixed it. He was visiting, and we were talking about my plans. He asked if I'd like to sign on as a ship's boy. First of all I thought it was a good idea – because of the travelling, see? Then I wasn't so sure. I'd rather have worked in a garage. With engines. Cars and engines, that's what I like. But then Uncle Ben came out with the *Almax Venturer* offer there and then, and I only had three days to think it over. My mum and dad were all for it, because of the *Almax Venturer* only going along the coast. They wouldn't have let me go overseas. I think they're scared I'll fall madly

18

in love with some woman on the other side of the world.'

'A wife in every port,' said John MacGraw, grinning.

'Isn't that right, then?'

'Not on your pay!' chuckled John MacGraw. 'No, seriously, most of the men on the *Almax Venturer* are married, and they get shore-leave after six weeks aboard. Anyone can hold out that long.'

'I reckon two days is too long for me,' said Peter. 'Because of the seasickness, I mean,' he added hastily.

'It'll pass over,' said John. 'Come down to the galley. Time for coffee.'

Peter followed John into the mess.

About half a dozen men were sitting at several tables. Most of them hardly looked up as John and Peter came in. Peter had forgotten their names, except for Beagles, the first mate.

John made his way over to a table where two men in blue work-clothes were already sitting: they were deck-hands, like John and Peter, except that Peter ranked lower.

'Andy,' grunted John, by way of greeting. 'Len.'

The two men nodded.

'Plenty of tea here,' said Andy.

John sat down. Peter followed suit.

'Hungry?' asked Len, with a knowing smile.

Peter shook his head and pressed his lips together. The thought of food turned him right over.

'If you don't eat something soon the flesh'll fall off your bones,' grinned Andy. 'Things aren't what they used to be. Ship's cats and ship's boys used to be as fat as barrels.'

Peter joined in the laughter. The men weren't

19

going to treat him with kid-gloves; he was new. John had warned him. Newcomers were always fair game as a target for old jokes.

Peter drank some tea, without milk or sugar. It was all he could manage to get down.

Two more men soon came over to their table: Bruce and Sam, who were deck-hands too. Finally the bo'sun, Bert Taylor, joined them. He was their immediate superior and assigned them their jobs. All orders from the bridge came through him. Peter had the feeling he was not particularly popular, but he decided he would form his own opinion of the man.

'Well, you can do something to earn your pay today, boys,' said Mr Taylor. 'Tanks Six and Twelve need scrubbing out.'

John MacGraw swore out loud. 'They might have thought of that before! We're coming in to Kingfish this evening, and if I know the guys on Kingfish they'll want to see us off again as soon as possible. That's bound to mean a night shift.'

'Complain to Beagles. He told me five minutes ago. If I'd known before I could have told you before, right? We don't have much time. Everyone'll have to muscle in. Including Little Titch.'

Peter felt the blood rise to his cheeks. 'Peter,' he said firmly. 'My name's Peter.'

The bo'sun looked him up and down in surprise. He frowned, and leaned slightly forward. 'When I was a ship's boy,' he said quietly, 'the bo'sun would have tanned my hide for that. Don't you ever try it again, you hear? I'm not having any little smart Aleck cheek me. Not even if his uncle's name *is* Ben Lexon.'

Peter had never liked quarrels, but if he gave in now it would drag on for ever. 'I wasn't cheeking you,' he said, trying to keep fear out of his voice.

20

'I only wanted you to call me by my real name. I mean, I call you by *your* real name.'

Andy chuckled. 'Just call him Killer! That's what he's known as. Hits the nail right on the head, eh? Ask him how he got the name, why don't you?'

The men laughed. The bo'sun relaxed, but the cold look did not leave his eyes. 'Five minutes,' he said, looking at the time. 'I'll open the manhole on the stern deck. Get your lungs full of fresh air while you can.'

He rose and strode quickly to the exit.

'The calculating swine,' said Andy, out loud. 'Bet you he did know earlier.'

Bruce shook his head. 'I was there when Beagles told him. He was just as surprised as you.'

'I don't like the guy all the same,' said Andy, forcefully.

John stopped him with an impatient gesture. 'Don't you wonder why this sudden hurry?' he asked. 'Plans were for us to take on oil just for Hastings. It's never been above five thousand for Hastings. So why would we be needing Tanks Six and Twelve? They've been empty for months, as far as I know.'

The men looked thoughtfully at each other.

'A full ship,' said Andy, finally. 'Who's it for?'

'I'll ask Taylor,' said John. 'Come on, let's go. The five minutes are up.'

The bo'sun was waiting for them on the quarter-deck. He had raised the cover of the manhole. The round opening was hardly big enough to let a man through.

Peter looked down. The light did not reach the bottom. All he could see was an iron ladder and part of the side of the tank.

'Andy, Len and Little Titch can do this tank,

and the rest of you begin on Number Twelve.'

'Peter's staying with me,' said John firmly. 'You know the rules, Taylor. The ship's boy works with the longest-serving deck-hand. That's me.'

The bo'sun took a deep breath, as if squaring up for a tough fight, but then thought better of it. 'Bruce, you work with Andy and Len, and Little Titch here can stay with John.'

'Peter,' said John, harshly. 'That's what he asked you to call him, Taylor. His name's Peter.'

The bo'sun straightened up. He was as tall and heavy as John MacGraw.

'One of these days you'll open your big mouth so wide you'll fall right in it, John. Yeah, I know you were offered the bo'sun's job before me, but you turned it down and I took it. So that's all clear, right? Or do I have to get all orders signed by the first mate from now on?'

'This isn't anything to do with all that,' said John. 'This is just a question of good manners.'

'I'll talk any way I like. And if Little Titch can't take it he shouldn't have signed on a ship. Now, get moving. We've wasted enough time already.'

John turned away without a word. Peter and Sam followed him.

'He's no good,' said John, more to himself than to his two companions. 'Maybe I really did make a mistake . . . '

Peter would have liked to know what John meant by that, but as Sam made no comment, neither did he.

He followed John to an exit amidships, and then down some narrow steps to the first lower deck down. The door of the big stowage room was open. It was the largest on the *Almax Venturer*, apart, of course, from the tanks.

22

Against one wall stood a lathe, a workbench with all kinds of tools, and a large iron welding bench. The rest of the room was full of shelves, neatly stacked with assorted items of equipment, tools and spare parts.

'You take the hose trolley,' John told Peter. He himself picked up three large, shallow breathing tanks: they were not oxygen equipment of the kind used by divers, but tanks with chemical filters to remove harmful gases from the air. They were made of plastic and very lightweight.

John handed out protective waterproof suits made of yellow plastic, which the men put on over their work clothes. There was only a narrow slit for the eyes, and they would cover that later with the masks of their breathing apparatus.

'Why go to all this bother?' asked Peter.

'It's filthy dirty down there,' Sam told him. 'Oil sticks to the metal like a thick crust. The automatic sprays can't deal with it. You have to use a concentrated jet of water from a hosepipe.'

'But what's the breathing equipment for?'

'The oil's giving off gases all the time. Sometimes gas pockets form. A single spark would explode them. Us too. It's gas you've got to watch out for, laddie. Crude oil itself doesn't burn easily as long as it's not heated.'

Peter felt sweat trickling down his neck. 'It's warm in these things,' he said, though in fact he was sweating with fear.

'Put the mask on,' said John. 'It'll help you get used to the breathing apparatus.'

Peter pulled the headband on and put the mask in place.

'Got it on properly?'

Peter nodded, and Sam opened a valve in the backpack.

He could breathe again, but it was some time before the resistance stopped bothering him.

Then they were ready. Sam stayed up on the top deck, to keep a watch and pay the hose out.

John went down into the tank first. He held on to the ladder with one hand and pulled the hose along with the other. He had a powerful torch hanging round his neck; its light wandered aimlessly over the walls of the tank.

Peter followed a few paces behind him. He was carrying a torch too. As he had a hand free, he could direct its beam.

There were butterflies in his stomach; the smell was stupefying even through the mask of the breathing apparatus. For a moment he felt panic rise like a wall in his chest, but the air he was breathing was pure.

The downward climb seemed to last for ever. The sound of their boots on the iron rungs echoed back from the walls, unnaturally loud.

John was waiting at the foot of the steps. The tank was much narrower at the bottom than the top, and Peter could make out the curve of its side quite clearly.

He shone his torch over the walls. The space inside the tank was considerably more cramped than he had thought. There was a clear view of its full height only along the ladder by which they had reached the bottom. The rest of the tank was criss-crossed with countless transverse and vertical iron struts. They were thicker than railway lines, and interspersed with fist-sized rivets.

John shone his torch on a small opening in the side wall.

'That way,' he said. Peter could hardly make out his voice through the mask of the breathing apparatus.

John pulled the hose along behind him by its nozzle. Peter was holding it too, a little farther back.

The opening in the side wall was so low that they had to crawl through on all fours. Peter could feel the muddy slurry on the floor through his rubber gloves. They reached a second chamber, exactly like the first. There was another opening here, leading to the third and last chamber. John shone his torch on several valves on the side walls. 'For the ballast water,' he said. Then he showed Peter the well – a large, round depression in the floor where the water collected and was then pumped back into the sea. Innumerable clusters of pipes ran across the upper part of the tank. Most of them were for carrying air away, but some branched and ran straight down. These had intake sockets at every level, and the oil was pumped in through them.

The viscous crude oil had left traces everywhere. The smooth walls were relatively clean, but there was a thick sediment in many places between the struts and in the numerous corners.

'We'll start with the top half,' said John. They had to climb another ladder to a narrow platform roughly in the middle of the tank.

John propped the nozzle against the wall like a mortar, and then pulled on the control line which ran along the hose.

'Hold on there, as hard as you can,' said John, pointing to the part of the hose at the base of the nozzle.

The water came out with great force. The hose

began to move as if it were alive. Then it stiffened, and water shot violently out of the nozzle. John directed the jet on to the pipes under the deck. It cut through the encrusted oil like a knife, peeling it away in great flakes.

They worked for an hour in silence. First the deck, then the walls, working from top to bottom, until they had finished the first chamber. In the second chamber, John got Peter to hold the nozzle. The boy's arms were soon aching with the pressure it exerted on him.

It was not an easy job.

By the time they had finished the last chamber Peter was so exhausted that he almost fell off the ladder as they climbed back to the top deck.

'Whew!' breathed John, tearing the mask of the breathing apparatus off his face. 'Thank God that's over! Enjoy yourself?'

Peter was sitting on the deck, his arms heavy as lead. The daylight dazzled him.

'How often?' he asked.

John and Sam laughed heartily. 'Too often,' said Sam at last.

They were through with the tanks at three o'clock. The tools were put away, the protective suits hung up to dry. They had missed the mid-day meal, but John said that was nothing unusual. The mess was always open, and the jobs that had to be done couldn't be kept waiting because of regular mealtimes. There was just one rule on a tanker: keep going, don't lose time, not a minute, keep on moving. Everyone had to observe that rule, from the ship's boy to the captain.

They saw the tender on their way to the mess: a small vessel of two or three thousand tons. She was swiftly coming closer.

'For us?' Sam sounded surprised.

John nodded. 'See the flag she's flying? It means "Coming alongside".'

They stood there for a while watching the tender. Beagles, the first mate, stood on the outer bridge, working the shutter of a signal light. The answer flashed back from the bridge of the tender.

'Something funny about all this,' said John, thoughtfully. 'A full cargo, and now the tender. Looks like a long voyage. This time I really am going to get some information out of Taylor.'

They were alone in the mess. The cook had met them on their way there. 'Help yourselves,' he had said. 'It's all ready on the counter. I've got to organise the reloading.'

'What the hell's going on around here?' John had asked.

But the cook impatiently dismissed his question. 'The old man's going to speak to everyone personally.'

'Big deal,' muttered Sam.

As always, the food was good, even though it had been keeping warm for some time. The cook had worked in a first class hotel for years and he knew his trade. Good food was important: it was the crew's only form of entertainment while they were at sea.

They were still sitting around the table when the captain came into the mess. He was tall and tanned like a film star; there was a rumour among the men that he dyed his hair grey. He was sixty, but didn't look it. No one could remember ever hearing him raise his voice.

'I was going to have a word with you three earlier,' said Captain Thomson, greeting them, 'but you were busy with Tank Twelve. You did a good job too,' he added. 'Now, there's been a change to our schedule. As you know, we were supposed to be going to Hastings with five thousand tons. The company let me know today that we're loading fifty thousand, and our destination is now Rotterdam.'

There was a moment's silence, broken only by Sam, who expelled the air from his lungs as if whistling.

'Naturally the company will pay overseas allowances, and extra bonuses for overtime if we don't complete the voyage in the duration of your usual shift. I'll leave you to make up your own minds. Anyone who wants to sign off can go back with the tender and join the next shift in five weeks. We should be back again by then. However, I'll need your decision at once, so that I can tell the men on the other shift. Nobody's declined yet,' he added, with a hint of a smile.

'It'll take rather more than five weeks,' said John. 'Well, I reckon I'll work my shift in the normal way. I'm extending my house – got the builders coming in when I'm next on shore-leave. I can use the bonuses too. You can count me in.'

'I'll stay,' said Sam.

'Peter?'

'I'm not sure . . . I don't know that my parents would like it.'

'I did have a word with Ben Lexon,' said Captain Thomson, 'and *he* had a word with your parents. They've got no objection, so it's up to you to decide.'

'Then I'll stay too.'

'Good,' said Captain Thomson, pleased. 'Then the crew's complete. The weather forecast's not too bad. An area of low pressure to the west. Once we're past that it'll be as calm as a duckpond.'

John and Sam laughed heartily. 'We've heard that one before,' said Sam. 'Usually turns out we're the ducks!'

'Oh, it won't be that bad,' Captain Thomson replied. 'We'll stick to the thirtieth parallel. With a bit of luck we'll catch the southern equatorial current and have the trade winds behind us. A pleasure cruise, that's what this will be.'

3

The sun was low in the west when they reached the first oil rig in Bass Strait.

John, Sam and Peter were sitting behind one of the big winches on the foreship. It was their off-duty watch, and John and Sam were surreptitiously smoking. Smoking was strictly forbidden anywhere on deck, but there were no ventilation hatches on the foredeck, and the winch gave enough cover to conceal them from anyone on the bridge looking that way.

'Tunny,' said John, pointing to the oil platform. 'And out there you can just see the top of Flounder. Then it's Mackerel and Kingfish. Sixteen oilfields, all called after fish.'

They were going at only half speed. Since reaching the oil-fields off Ninety Mile Beach they had kept passing other tankers. John and Sam knew almost all of them by sight.

The two derricks of the *Almax Venturer* swung out and lowered their couplings to the loading raft. They acted as links between the oil pipelines of the platform and those of the ship. There were six of them in all, and by the time the last was closed crude oil was already flowing through the first. Every minute meant money.

30

By now the small motorboat had reached the tanker's bows.

John waved to the two men. 'Hi, Paul. Hi, Tony. How's it going?'

'Not so bad. We come off shift in a couple of weeks' time. Then it's eight weeks' shore-leave. Envious?'

John laughed. 'Only of your pay, Paul.'

'I don't know what you've got to grouse about, John! You're getting a free trip to Europe, right?'

'I'll swap with you!' called John.

Paul shook his head, laughing. 'It's true what they're saying on Kingfish, then? You're bound for Europe?'

'Yes.'

'I hope it'll be worth your while!'

John shrugged his shoulders. 'Not my business, Paul. I guess the Almax people know what they're doing. Nobody asked us! Going to make us fast now, or just sit around passing the time of day.'

'Ready when you are. Where's the line?'

John threw the coiled line down into the motorboat. Paul tied the end of it around one of the hooks on the nearest anchor buoy.

By now Sam had connected a thick cable to the line through a sliding eyelet. The heavy cable slipped along the line and was then made fast to the anchor buoy by the two men in the motorboat. Sam pulled it taut with a winch.

They fastened two more cables to anchor buoys. These, together with the cables at the stern, held the *Almax Venturer* in an iron grip that scarcely gave at all in a medium swell.

The tanker was made fast, the pumps were working to full capacity. There was nothing more for John, Sam and Peter to do just now.

Sam and John went into the mess to watch a film on TV. It was their last chance. Later, the distance from the mainland would be too great, and they would have to make do with videos.

Peter stood at the rail until darkness fell over the ship and the oil rig. Suddenly the night was full of lights. The red marker lights of the shipping channels were winking everywhere. The oil rigs looked like Christmas trees, with the headlights of a number of tankers moving between them. The *Almax Venturer* herself was brightly illuminated, particularly amidships, where powerful floodlights bathed the masts supporting the loading gear and the coupling pipes in glistening silvery light.

It was a mild night, with only a slight breeze blowing from the mainland.

Peter breathed deeply. His nausea had almost gone now. Only a faint echo of it gnawed away in his stomach, like a warning that it might be back anytime. Well, he'd survive. He felt strong enough now. The worst was over: his first day, with his fears about the ship, the sea and the men. This was his third day. Soon he would be a part of the ship, like the others. For the first time he found himself looking forward to the voyage to Europe. He glanced up at the bridge. In the brightly lit wheelhouse he saw the figure of the second mate, who was responsible for seeing that the oil was evenly distributed in the tanks. A single mistake in his calculations could rip the ship apart. The *Almax Venturer* was not a new vessel. However, she was equipped with computers to work out the best possible distribution of her cargo.

The pumps worked on ceaselessly. Their humming and the quiet singing of the kilometres of pipelines on the *Almax Venturer* were the men's

32

constant companions day and night. They never really got used to them. Only when the wind rose did the sound die down a little. But the smell was always with them, and never got any less. Even on shore-leave they could smell the oil in their hair and their clothes.

While they were lying off Kingfish 1 the weather changed. It was not one of the dreaded sudden falls in atmospheric pressure which occur so often in the Tasman Sea. The sky stayed clear. Only the wind freshened, turning from north to south-west. The colour of the sea changed to vivid green, and all of a sudden the waves were capped with white foam.

After twenty-four hours the *Almax Venturer* was loaded right up to her deck. Peter had been sent to the foreship again as they cast off. This time he was operating a winch and winding in one of the three retaining cables. Paul and Tony, who had helped them make fast, were in the motorboat again.

'Hey, John!' shouted Paul. 'You're over the Plimsoll line.'

'How far over?'

'Couple of hand's-breadths.'

John swore.

'Have a good trip,' Paul called. 'And good luck! You'll be needing it!'

John dismissed the idea, laughing. 'I'd trust the *Almax Venturer* anywhere!' he shouted back.

The little motorboat was moving away fast.

'Here we go,' said Sam, and at almost the same moment the deck plates began to quiver as the propellers bored into the water.

It was a long time before the fully loaded giant finally got under way, adjusting to the violent shuddering set up by the regular vibration of the drive shafts. Once loaded, the *Almax Venturer* was a different vessel: more submarine than surface craft. Three-quarters of her hull was under water now, there was more resistance, and she was displacing much more water. The engines had to work harder, consuming more fuel, and yet they were now going eight knots slower.

The way the ship moved had changed too. She reacted much more sluggishly to the steering and the waves. Whereas before she had been bobbing on the waves like a cork, she now ploughed through the water like a bit of flotsam. And although the sea was not very high, a few waves were already washing over the deck.

'What did Paul mean about the Plimsoll line?' asked Peter.

'Did you notice the draft gauge on the bows? All those lines? The Plimsoll line is the one with the small circle. It means the ship shouldn't sink any lower. You could call it the upper load line.'

'And we're above it?' asked Peter.

John laughed. 'Oh, the *Almax Venturer* can cope! No one sticks exactly to the rule. Depends how warm it is, you see. When we get into warmer waters we'll ride higher. Don't ask me why, but that's how it is.'

The *Almax Venturer* was going due west now. The voyage had begun. The west wind blew into the men's faces like tiny cold needles, pricking deeper as the hours went by.

'The Roaring Forties,' said John. 'Those are the freezing winds straight from the South Pole. It'll soon be blowing like an icy hell out here.'

The clouds raced across the sky as if to fall upon the *Almax Venturer*. John's group began putting out storm-lines, several lines fixed along the rail. John

34

showed Peter how to fasten them. It was not an easy job. The wind was strong now, and the waves high enough to set the *Almax Venturer* pitching. They began to work on the quarterdeck behind the superstructure, fastening the lines every ten feet. If the bad weather continued they would lay transverse lines across the deck as well.

They had secured about half the port side when the bo'sun came striding over to them. 'What the hell do you lot think you're doing here?' he asked, angrily. But it was John he was looking at.

John straightened up slowly. 'Fixing storm-lines, Taylor, can't you see?'

'Who said to?'

'We'll be right in the storm in an hour's time. I don't need any other orders.'

'You listen to me, MacGraw!' hissed the bo'sun, red in the face. 'I've had enough of you and your insubordination. This time I'm reporting it to the Captain. I give the orders around here.'

John was unperturbed. 'What are you on about, Taylor? You know your trade as well as I do. The storm-lines have to be fixed, right? So we both want the same thing, okay? You don't have to keep proving you're the bo'sun.'

The bo'sun returned John's glance with one of grim fury. 'I'll get you yet, MacGraw,' he snarled, and then turned away.

'What's the matter with him?' asked Peter.

'Oh, it's an old quarrel between us,' said John. 'We once sailed on another ship together. I was bo'sun then and he was a deck-hand. He made a mistake and I got him fired. It's that simple. If he gets a chance he'll have me fired too. But he'll have to wait a long time,' added John, laughing.

35

'Why did you turn the job of bo'sun on the *Almax Venturer* down when you could have had it?' asked Peter.

'That's a long story,' said John, clamming up. Peter was about to ask another question, but he saw Sam shaking his head slightly.

The storm got to them in the middle of the night. The wind howled around the superstructure, and the sea was rumbling like machinery. Peter clung to the frame of his bunk with both hands. He dared not put the light on; he was afraid he would fall out of the bunk as soon as he let go of its side.

The ship pitched and rolled, and Peter noticed for the first time how many ways she could move at once. He tried to sit up, but all of a sudden the world seemed to tip downwards, at a slanting angle. He hit his head against something hard, and cursed.

'What's up?' asked John, drowsily.

Peter was glad to be sharing a cabin with John MacGraw. John was often brusque, to the other men as well as to him, but he was always fair, and didn't keep cracking jokes at the boy's expense.

Peter found the light switch. 'What's up?' John repeated.

'How can you sleep?'

'Easy! You didn't wake me up just to ask me that, did you?'

'Sorry,' said Peter.

'Okay,' grunted John. 'Your first storm, right? I can still remember *my* first storm. God, that's a long time ago. I was on a small ship then. I was sure we were going to drown – paralysed with fright, I was! Literally. The bo'sun had to box my ears before I could move. And I'm still here. That's the proof of the pudding, okay? The storm'll pass over. The *Almax Venturer*'s been through worse than this.'

Peter smiled uncertainly. 'Isn't there anything we ought to do?'

'Like what? Pouring oil on the waters? The storm will last just as long as the wind likes. Doesn't make any difference if you're asleep or awake. Someone's steering up on the bridge. If they need help they'll call us.'

'It's just that the bo'sun said I'd better be ready for a long watch.'

John raised himself on his elbows and looked hard at Peter. 'It's time we had a talk, son. You've been aboard nearly a week, you've seen how things are here. So long as we all do our job the officers don't bother us, and it's about time Taylor got used to that idea. The days of the old martinets with their cat-o'-nine-tails are gone.'

Peter laughed. 'Cat-o'-nine-tails?'

'Kind of whip, sonny. And believe me, they used it.'

'But Taylor's my boss.'

'Mine too. There's an old rule on shipboard: the eldest deck-hand takes the ship's boy in tow. That used to mean the boy would have to do all his dirty work for him. These days it simply means I teach you all the tricks of the trade. You have any problems, you bring them to me.'

'Okay,' said Peter.

'And now try to get some sleep. It's twice as hard working in a high sea. If you really fall behind on your sleep you'll never make it up.'

So saying, John turned to the wall and fell asleep at once. But Peter could not sleep. He left the light on above his bunk. It wouldn't bother John.

The storm was raging as strongly as ever. It flung

37

wave after wave against the *Almax Venturer* as she ploughed on through the swirling chaos. The impact of tons of water echoed dully through the whole ship. The wind tore at the superstructure as if it were a sail, and spray and rain lashed the metal with a sound like pebbles rattling.

Peter wished the cabin had a porthole so that he could see the storm.

He did not know how long he had been lying awake. He nodded off several times, and then another jolt would jerk him out of sleep again. Suddenly he felt a hand shaking him roughly by the shoulder.

'Wake up, kid! I've got a job for you.'

Peter sat up, drowsily. The bo'sun stood there, grinning. He was wearing red oilskins and the regulation safety helmet, with the firm's name, Almax, above his forehead. Water was dripping from his clothes and collecting on the floor in little puddles.

'Come on!' said the bo'sun. 'I'll see you on the foredeck in five minutes. I'll be waiting by the exit gangway.'

John murmured restlessly and turned on his other side.

'Is John coming too?' asked Peter.

The bo'sun's grin widened. 'Let Mummy have her nice sleep!' he mocked. 'Time for little boys to go to work.' And, before Peter could reply, he had turned and marched out of the cabin.

Peter dressed quickly. His fingers were shaking. He did not know whether he ought to wake John. He wanted to, but the bo'sun's jeering still echoed in his ears. He hoped, up to the last minute, that John would wake of his own accord, but he did not. Shutting the door behind him, he went along the gangway, arms outstretched to balance himself against the moving of the ship.

The bo'sun was waiting for him at the exit, by the doorway to the deck. There was a pane of glass in the top of the door. The wind was flinging rain and spray almost horizontally at it.

'It's the ship's boat on the foredeck,' said the bo'sun. 'The wind's torn the tarpaulin off it. Get it back on.'

Taylor had to lean his whole weight against the door to get it open. Instantly, Peter was wet through. He bent his head and followed the bo'sun up the gangway to the deck. They moved sideways, so as to offer as little resistance as possible to the wind. Peter grabbed the rail with both hands.

The bo'sun stopped. Peter looked up for the first time.

Ahead of him, two hundred metres of foredeck was rearing up to meet the storm. 'My God!' he exclaimed.

The bo'sun laughed soundlessly.

The deck rose and fell beneath their feet like a lift. Half of it was under water. White foam eddied as if the sea were boiling. Whenever the bows plunged into a particularly large wave the water shot up like a vast fountain. Now and then the *Almax Venturer* rolled violently sideways, as if to fling the masses of water angrily off her back, and then another wave would come washing over the deck again.

The floodlights cast long white fingers of light on the deck. 'Off you go,' said the bo'sun.

Peter looked at the ship's boat. It seemed a very long way off, and the flooded deck was between him and it. 'I can't.'

'Get on with it, boy. This isn't a Sunday School

treat.' The bo'sun's voice lost some of its harshness. 'Look, we've all had to face what we don't fancy some time or other. This job isn't as bad as it looks. Nothing to it, believe you me.'

'Okay,' Peter said. 'But I'm not going alone.'

The bo'sun thought that over. 'I'll stay behind you till we reach the sailroom hatch. After that you're on your own.'

Peter clutched the storm-line farthest from the rail and then made his way slowly forward. He was inching his way along – whatever happened he didn't want to let go of the line.

He had no idea whether the bo'sun was following him. It didn't matter any more. He was alone. He knew it was not the sea he was fighting. He was fighting fear, and no one could help him with that.

Peter dared not look out at the raging sea. If he raised his eyes he felt sure he would be done for. It was the longest walk of his life. The wet rope rubbed against his chest, and the cascades of water streaming over the deck tugged at his boots.

He stopped four times, each time beside one of the floodlights, which seemed like islands of safety in the darkness of the storm. Once he looked back. The bo'sun was not following. He felt both rage and relief, almost a sense of elation, and if it hadn't been an idiotic thing to do he would have sung out loud in the lashing rain. It was over. His fear had left him. His anger was his victory over the bo'sun who had sent him out to torment him with his own fear. In the end he had beaten both his fears and the bo'sun.

He heard the tarpaulin of the ship's boat long before he got there. It was flapping violently in the wind, up and down, with a loud report like a whipcrack.

40

Peter still clung to the storm-line, but he was making better progress now.

He waited level with the ship's boat until the bows rose on the crest of a wave, and then he ran for it – only five metres, but he had nothing to hold on to.

Clinging to the ship's boat with one hand, he caught the tarpaulin with the other and lashed it to the side of the boat. The job took him barely ten minutes, but he couldn't have lasted much longer. His hands were cold, and his fingers numb and stiff.

He waited for another suitable wave before running for the security of the storm-line again.

On the way back he looked up at the bridge. He saw figures moving behind the big glass panes, but he was too far off to recognise them.

He went cautiously, but his hands were as cold as ice and their grip was weaker now. The ship bucked beneath him. He reacted automatically to the movement by bending his knees. But somehow or other the tanker was turning a different way now, and suddenly he lost his hold on the storm-line. A dozen metres ahead of him a breaker crashed to the deck, pouring over it like frothy beer. It was taller than any of the other waves so far. As it reached Peter the *Almax Venturer* was on her way down into the next trough, and its force carried him helplessly away. He was to remember every detail later.

There was just one clear thought in his head: the storm-lines. They had fixed them all over the deck. He just had to keep his hands down and wait for the water to carry him to one of them. The cold and wet cut into his body. He seemed to be slithering over the steel plates of the deck for ever. Then a sudden pain shot through his leg. He was gasping for breath, and the water was surging over him. The pain was so bad that at first he did not notice he was stuck.

When he could breathe again, he sat up, dizzily. His foot was jammed between the flange of a pipe and a ventilation hatch. He tried to twist it free, but found he could not move it.

He straightened up a little more, looking back at the superstructure. The bo'sun must have seen him.

Peter saw nothing but a black wall. The storm, the ship, the entire world seemed to be holding its breath for a second. Realisation struck him like a blow. The wall was a wave, taller and mightier than any he had seen yet. It was making for him, black with white eddies climbing up, higher and higher, as if they would never break. And in front of the wave came a shadowy shape, arms and legs balancing each other, skilful and sure.

A strong arm hauled him up. One jerk, and his foot was free.

His body was pressed against a winch.

'It's you!' gasped Peter, and then the wave had reached them and was surging over them both. He held his breath until he thought his lungs would burst.

'Quick!' ordered a voice, but before Peter could think straight he was being carried across the deck, into light and warmth.

'Why didn't you wake me up?' John asked.

'You were asleep. I thought . . . '

'Later,' John interrupted. 'That foot okay?'

Peter took a cautious step. 'Doesn't seem to be broken,' he said.

'Good. Go back to the cabin and have a shower. A thorough one, till your skin's tingling. And then go up to the bridge to have one of the officers take a look at your foot.'

'It's not that bad,' said Peter. 'Really.'

'Move!' John ordered, and only then did Peter see the bo'sun.

'Come here, Taylor,' said John.

Peter stayed where he was. 'Leave him alone, John,' he said. 'This is my business.'

The bo'sun laughed. 'Need the boy to protect you, eh?' he inquired.

'I said move!'

Slowly, Peter made his way down the steps. He heard nothing for a while, and then there was a grunt followed by the thud of a blow. The sound came several more times before Peter reached the cabin.

No one mentioned the incident again. Both John and the bo'sun bore obvious marks of the fight on their faces, but no questions were asked. Everyone had known it was coming; the actual reason didn't matter.

'Who won?' Peter asked that evening.

John laughed, face twisting with pain. 'No one.'

'A draw,' said Peter, disappointed.

'I didn't say that.'

'Then you did win!'

John smiled crookedly. 'If you're so keen to think so. When I left Taylor he was lying on the floor, not moving.'

'Good,' said Peter, pleased. 'I knew you could beat him.'

'Maybe,' said John, 'but he's not going to give up on that account. This isn't like a couple of kids fighting at school, you know. Taylor's tough. And he's no fool. He'll be sticking close to me after this. Look at it that way, and it was probably worth the effort. He'll leave *you* alone now.'

4

Friday, 9.00 hours

The depression in the west continued. The storm raged on as violently as ever, flinging wave after wave against the bows of the *Almax Venturer*, but she held her course.

They hoped daily for a break in the weather, searching the sky for signs of any change, but there was none. They were losing speed at the rate of five and sometimes eight knots.

By the time they reached one hundred and fifteen degrees east, they had left the Australian continent behind them.

'What's the weather forecast?' asked Captain Thomson.

Mr Hill, the third mate, put his cup down. 'No change. The long-term forecast says a slight improvement to the south is expected.'

'It's mainly the north that interests us,' Captain Thomson pointed out. 'How do things look there?'

'Not too good,' said the third mate. 'The storm front goes as far as the twenty-fifth parallel.'

'Not much of a pleasure cruise after all,' remarked Captain Thomson.

'Hardly,' agreed Mr Beagles.

Their conversation was taking place in the Captain's cabin. He had asked the first and third mates there

44

for a conference. This was unusual: normally they discussed their problems on the bridge.

Captain Thomson poured himself more coffee.

'Gentlemen,' he said, after a long pause, 'I have to make an important decision. That's why I asked you to come here. I'd like to have your opinion before I make up my mind, and this struck me as the best place. Too much coming and going on the bridge. I'll talk to Mr Brenagan personally later. I know I can count on your discretion.'

He brought out a piece of paper from under a file.

'Mr Hill received a coded radio message this morning. This is what it says in clear.'

He put the piece of paper on the table. The two officers leaned forward to read the brief text.

Please change course to south-south-west. Deviation ten degrees, weather permitting. Arrival time Rotterdam plus ten days. Extra pay and bonuses authorised. Almax.

The two men said nothing for quite a long time. Finally, Mr Beagles asked, 'What does it mean?'

'Oh, that's simple enough,' said Captain Thomson. 'They want us to delay our arrival. Oil prices must have risen again, so the later we get there, the more Almax will earn.'

'You want to slacken speed?' asked Mr Hill, the third mate.

'Not with the storm coming straight towards us. That'd be suicide.'

'Then we'll have to change course,' said Mr Beagles.

'Exactly. The radio message suggests south-south-west. That would make the voyage almost ten days longer.'

'And Almax would make a much higher profit,' added Mr Beagles.

'Yes, that's the idea,' agreed Captain Thomson, 'but so far as I'm concerned it's not the main consideration. No one can expect me to run straight into this storm. Whatever happens I've got to change course to go around it.'

'Why not north?' asked Mr Hill.

'You think that would be a good idea?' asked Captain Thomson.

The third mate looked at his notes, hesitating. 'I'm not sure,' he said, uncertainly. 'The storm front does reach far north, but it's not much better to the south. We have the west wind right against us. The Roaring Forties are blowing straight in our face. No trade route runs so far south. We'd probably be the only vessel in an enormous area.'

Captain Thomson nodded thoughtfully.

'If you read the history of sea travel,' he said, 'you'll find the same problem coming up again and again. To a great many seamen, the fortieth parallel is still pretty much like the end of the world. I can't tell you why. As long as there are no ice floes I don't see any difficulty. I was on the southerly route for five years. In nineteen-forty to 'forty-five, when the Germans and Japanese were sinking anything that moved north of the Antarctic. Sometimes we went so far south we had to make our way through the pack ice. As you see, we survived. If my information's correct, our losses were no greater than on the traditional route. I suggest we change course to south-south-west until we're away from the storm, and then, weather permitting, turn back west-north-west. Agreed?'

'Agreed,' said Mr Beagles.

Mr Hill nodded in silence.

'Good,' said Captain Thomson. 'Thank you, gentlemen. I'm sure the crew will have no objection to a rather calmer voyage. I'll speak to them all myself about the extra time. Not that it makes any difference,' he added, smiling. 'None of them can decide not to sign on at this point! It's just a matter of morale. There's obviously been some kind of trouble between MacGraw and Taylor, though as usual, no one admits to knowing anything. Bad blood among the crew is worse than a storm; I'm gong to have a word with Taylor and MacGraw. Maybe I'll be able to persuade MacGraw to take on the job of bo'sun after all. He's the better man, no doubt about it. Taylor's not very popular with the crew; that's probably the reason for all this constant friction. It'll be high time for a change at the end of this voyage. And until then we must keep our ears and eyes open.'

5

Peter stretched out on his bunk. Every bone in his body was aching. 'What's the time?'

John yawned loudly before answering. 'Two and a half hours to go till the next watch,' he said.

That was the only thing that mattered now: the time between watches. The ship's constant movement made any job, however small, an almost impossible task. Even experienced deck-hands like John just wanted to lie down.

Peter stared up at the ventilation grille in the cabin ceiling. He counted its sections for the third time. He could have stayed lying there for ever. It was pleasantly warm in the cabin, and the movement of the ship didn't seem quite so bad.

'Have you been at sea long, John?'

John laughed quietly. 'Too long,' he said. 'I went straight to sea from school, when I was twelve. There wasn't any unemployment then. I could have got any kind of job, but it was the sea I fancied. Too many adventure stories, that was my trouble. I'd read all these stories about ships and voyages of discovery. No wonder I ended up believing them, eh?'

'If that's how you felt, why did you stick at it? You could have found another job ages ago if you didn't like this one.'

48

'I didn't say I didn't like it. Only it's a sight less romantic than I'd thought. Most of the time we were slaving away for our pay. Don't get me wrong – I'm not complaining. I'd never earn as much on shore. Since supertankers came in the oil companies have paid top wages. That's why I can't get out now. I only have to say the word and there'll be someone else ready to snap up my job. There's a waiting list from here to eternity. No, I'm staying. Another ten years and then I'll retire. I'll have paid off my mortgage by then. Might move house, at that. Up to the mountains. I've had enough of water. I guess I might like the mountains, so long as it's not too cold. I sometimes dream of it, you know. When I'm on watch. I dream of a nice open fire and my wife fussing over me.'

'You're married?' asked Peter, surprised. 'You never told me. I was sure you were a bachelor.'

'Oh, well,' said John, in some embarrassment. 'Nothing wrong with being married, is there?'

'Of course not,' Peter hastened to say. 'I was surprised, that's all.'

John muttered something inaudible. 'We'll keep it between the two of us, okay?' he added out loud.

'What?'

'You know – me being married.'

Peter laughed. 'It's not a secret, is it?' he said.

'It is here.'

'Why?'

'It just is.'

'Oh, come on! There must be some reason.'

'Well, it's Sam and Andy, that's all,' John told him. 'I mean, if they find out, they won't want me with them when we go on shore any more. They're not married, see? Got a way with the women, Sam has – only has to smile and they melt like butter. How about you?' he added quickly. 'Got a girl friend?'

'There's Sue,' said Peter. 'But she's not a real girl friend. We write to each other. She used to live in the same street, and then she moved. So now we write.'

'Ah, well, you've got plenty of time,' said John. 'Going to stay with the *Almax Venturer*?'

'I'm not sure. Right now I'm only on a try-out period. I guess I won't make my mind up till we get back. Three years is a long time.'

'Only when you're fifteen,' remarked John. 'At my age, a year's nothing.'

'What would you do if you were me?'

'Well, it's never easy to make someone else's mind up,' said John. 'But I reckon I'd stay on. You can work with engines here too, you know. You could end up in the engine room – chief engineer. I've met a lot of men that started on something quite different from what they're doing now. It doesn't really matter where you begin – it's what you make of it that counts in the long run. Or that's what I think.'

'I've been in the engine room,' said Peter. 'I don't think I could work in there. The noise and heat would send me crazy.'

John was silent for a while. 'Ever see that film about the sinking of the *Titanic*?' he asked.

'I may have,' said Peter, surprised. 'On TV. Why?'

'I always think of it when I'm in the engine room. The bit where the *Titanic*'s engine room gets flooded and the boilers explode. The engine room always gets hit first. You're a prisoner down there. Up on deck at least you have a chance. Though I'd never jump in the water. Can't swim.'

'Honest?'

'Of course. Sam can't either. Nor Bruce. I don't know about the others. Wouldn't surprise me if half the crew can't swim.'

'That sounds really weird! On a ship.'

'Why? We're hired to work on board – the *Almax Venturer* does our swimming for us. Don't kid yourself: if you go overboard here you haven't a hope. We're much too near the Antarctic. The water's so cold you'd freeze in minutes.'

Peter shuddered. 'I'd rather not think about it,' he said. 'Though I do sometimes wonder what it'd be like. If we sank, I mean.'

John laughed. 'Well, you can practise this afternoon. Fire drill. It's Beagles' hobbyhorse. He knows his stuff, but he takes it too far sometimes. Once we all had to take to the boats – that was in the Tasman Sea, with waves as high as a house. Simulating it wasn't good enough for him. We had to get the boats into the water and several hundred metres away from the *Almax Venturer*. Captain Thomson nearly lost his entire crew. Only one of the boats had an engine, and that wouldn't start. It was a hell of a job getting us all back on board.'

'I hope we don't have to take to the boats today,' said Peter, shivering.

'Anything's possible,' grinned John. 'You never know where you are with Beagles.'

The fire drill was fixed for one p.m. Peter and John came out of the mess.

'Storm's slackened off a bit,' said John, glancing critically at the grey sky.

'The waves have changed direction,' said Peter.

'Don't be daft – the swell always goes the same way here.'

51

'No, really. Look at the bows. We're not going straight into the waves any more. They're to one side of us now. Didn't you notice we're not pitching so much?'

John stood still in surprise. 'Dammit, you're right! But it's not the swell, son. We've changed course.' He dug Peter in the ribs. 'Stormy petrels,' he said.

Peter followed the direction of his glance. He saw large black and white birds flying along beside the ship, close to the water.

'Cook's probably thrown some scraps of food overboard,' said John.

The birds were uttering loud, abrupt cries. Their numbers kept growing until they formed a living cloud. Suddenly a dozen or so white shapes shot out of their midst.

'Albatrosses,' said John, spitting disgustedly on the deck.

'What's the matter?' exclaimed Peter. 'They're amazing! Just look at their wing span. I'd say it was at least three metres. And see how they soar! Better than any plane.'

'Blasted birds,' muttered John, with dislike.

'Why?'

'Did you see their eyes? That fixed stare. As if they were picking their next victim.'

Peter laughed. 'You're not trying to kid me they're man-eaters?'

'Birds of death,' said John, seriously. 'Any ship they follow is doomed to sink. Storm birds, lad – they bring the storm with them.'

'That just has to be superstition,' said Peter. 'You can't really believe it!'

'Don't I, though? Albatrosses mean bad luck. Any seaman knows that.'

Peter shook his head in disbelief.

The albatrosses soared low, close to the deck of the *Almax Venturer*. Their mighty wings were outstretched, motionless, and their heads were thrust steadily forwards. Like gliders, thought Peter. And so close you could have put out a hand to reach them.

John guessed Peter's thoughts. 'Don't touch 'em, lad.'

'More superstition?'

'No, I mean it. In the old days sailors sometimes killed an albatross. None of them ever survived – their ships are at the bottom of the sea.'

'Serves them right,' said Peter. 'But seriously – you don't really believe those stories, do you?'

John shook his head. 'Not literally, maybe, but those birds still bring bad luck, you mark my words!'

The albatrosses accompanied them for several hours. Their big, black eyes stared fixedly, expressionlessly at the men.

Towards evening, they had run out of the storm. The swell rolled gently and harmlessly against the ship's side. The wind slackened, and the first clear patches appeared in the cloudy sky.

During the day, Captain Thomson spoke to all the men. No one seemed particularly surprised to hear about the ten extra days, although it might just have been that they were all glad to have the storm behind them.

John was the only one who seemed bothered. 'Hear that, son?' he said, as they were putting the tools away in the stowage room after fire drill.

'What?'

'She's moaning.'

'Who is?'

'The *Almax Venturer*. Can't you hear it?'

Peter listened to the noises of the ship. He could hear nothing out of the ordinary. 'You're still thinking of those albatrosses,' he said. 'You have to admit the weather's improved.'

'I'm not talking about the weather,' said John, impatiently. 'I'm talking about the ship. She's moaning, I tell you.'

'Oh, come off it!' snapped Peter. 'You've been in a funny mood all afternoon.'

'I know what I'm talking about,' John snapped back. 'What do *you* know about anything after two weeks at sea?'

'Okay, okay. I'm not arguing.'

John muttered something under his breath, and they said no more about it. However, John's bad temper did not improve.

Next morning the sky was clear. It was bitterly cold on deck, and the sun was hidden in milky mists. The albatrosses had disappeared. Only stormy petrels still flew over the ship. The crew put on fur jackets, hats and thick gloves, which got in the way whenever they had a job to do.

There were long icicles hanging from a waste pipe, and several valves were frozen up.

Towards mid-day a shout of 'Ship in sight!' rang out over the deck. Within minutes, the whole crew had gathered by the port rail.

The ship rose slowly above the horizon line. First only her funnel, with its thin plume of vapour; then the superstructure slowly came into view, as if rising from the depths of the sea.

'An American vessel,' called Mr Hill from the outer deck. He was holding binoculars through which he could make out the flag at the stern of the approaching ship. 'About eight tons,' he added. 'Looks like an ice-breaker. Probably an exploration vessel from McMurdo Sound.'

By now the ship was close enough for the men at the rail to make out details for themselves. She was painted bright red. The paint was as fresh and spotless as the rest of her.

Her strong bows were those of an ice-breaker, with a flat nose which would bring the entire weight of the ship to bear against slabs of ice. Her stern was built like the stern of a landing craft. It could be let down all along its length, and would then form a bridge strong enough for lorries to drive over it.

After a while, they could read the lettering on the bows: the ship's name was the *US Antarctica*.

A signal light flashed from the bridge of the *US Antarctica*. 'It says, "Coming alongside",' said John, who understood the signal.

The ship described a wide arc as she approached the *Almax Venturer*. She was faster and easier to manoeuvre than the big tanker. Up on her bridge, her captain suited his speed to the tanker's. A man in a thick fur jacket appeared on the outer bridge. He was wearing sunglasses. Their lenses reflected the light like mirrors.

'Hi there, *Almax Venturer*!' he shouted through a megaphone. 'What are you doing so far south?'

Mr Beagles raised his own megaphone. 'Hi there, *US Antarctica*,' he replied. 'Getting away from a storm – it was with us up to 48° 35′. High seas, strong winds.'

'Yeah, we heard about that one,' the man on the *US Antarctica* called back. 'All the same, I wouldn't go much farther south if I were you. We've had drift ice up to 52°.'

'We plan to change course to west-north-west at the fiftieth parallel. No problems there?'

'Not as far as we know. The ice is drifting slowly, but if the wind rises it'll soon catch up with you.'

'We'll keep our eyes skinned. What's your course?'

'West-north-west, like you, but we have to drop some homesick Aussies off in Perth first.'

'Keep as far east as you can. Maybe you'll avoid the storm that way.'

'Will do. What's your destination?'

'Rotterdam,' said Mr Beagles.

'Long way to go! Good luck, then.'

'Have a good trip,' called Mr Beagles.

The *US Antarctica* drifted slowly away from the *Almax Venturer*; then her engines began to roar, and she moved swiftly east. The crews of both vessels waved until they were out of sight of each other.

'Nice to know there's someone else around,' said Sam.

'Much help that'll be,' growled John. 'We'll be over a thousand kilometres apart within a day. Why, the South Pole's closer!'

'Ah, shut up, you old grouch!' said Sam. 'I don't know what's got into you all of a sudden. I mean, it's all for the best. Ten days' bonus pay comes to a nice little sum. I bet the builders'll be glad not to have you treading on their toes the whole time – your house will be finished when you get back.'

John muttered something and turned away. But Peter felt sure he had caught his remark.

'If we get back,' John had said.

6

The change in the weather came very suddenly.
Within an hour, the barometer fell by a hundred
and fifty millibars, and it went on falling. It was as
if a huge hole had suddenly opened up. They were
right in the middle of it, and it was just a question
of time before the whole world fell in.

For the first time, Peter realised what it actually
meant when people spoke of the calm before the
storm. It was a feeling, but a feeling so real you
could almost have reached out to touch it. The air
seemed laden with electricity, and every breath was
difficult.

There was not a cloud in sight, and yet the light
changed. The sky became much the same colour as the
sea, so that the water and horizon merged together.

John nodded gloomily, as if this was just what
he had expected.

All at once, the day changed to night. In the last
of the light, one of the men sighted a ship. They all
saw the flash of light refracted from a glass pane. But
when Mr Beagles looked through the telescope, it was
only a drifting ice floe.

The bo'sun put all the men on watch. He had
left Peter alone since his fight with John. They had
exchanged only the most essential words, but Peter

57

knew they weren't through with each other yet.

The men made all the hatches stormproof. The storm lines were still in place.

'Looks like a real brute,' said Sam.

'Will it be worse than the last storm?' Peter asked.

'You bet your life it will, kid. We're just about at the limit of navigable waters here. Farther on south there's drift ice, and then the pack ice. We never ought to have come so far south, that's what I say.'

'Hey, Sam!' called the bo'sun. 'Send the ship's boy over here!'

Peter looked around for John, but he was nowhere to be seen. The bo'sun was busy with the tarpaulin of the ship's boat. Peter thought it strange that he was the one the bo'sun wanted just now.

'Test the lines,' the bo'sun told him. 'And make sure everything's fast. You don't want another walk on deck in the middle of the night, I guess?'

Peter gritted his teeth. 'No.'

'Had an idea you didn't, Little Titch!'

He grinned provocatively, but Peter returned his glance calmly.

'Your mate has friends on the bridge,' said the bo'sun. 'You two make quite a pair. But I'm telling you now, influence there won't do you any good. If there's work to be done in this storm, you and he'll be the first to get wet. Understand?'

Peter shook his head. 'Look here, I've never done anything to harm you. You've no right to— '

The bo'sun's hand shot out as if to deliver a blow, but he only grabbed the collar of Peter's jacket.

'You never learn, do you, Little Titch?' he said. 'Don't talk to me about rights! My word goes around here.'

Peter was sure the bo'sun was about to hit him now. Then he saw John's face appear behind Taylor's back.

The bo'sun let go of him at once when he heard John's voice inquiring, 'Something wrong, Taylor?'

'Just having a little talk, man to man, MacGraw,' said the bo'sun, obviously spoiling for a fight. 'Nothing to do with you.'

'Take you on any time,' John offered. 'You've only got to say the word. I'll be happy to teach you another lesson.'

The bo'sun turned away in silence.

'One of these days I'll knock his teeth in,' said John, angrily. 'What did he want?'

'Nothing,' replied Peter. He was a poor liar, and he knew John saw through him.

'No more little walks on your own, Peter,' John said. 'There won't be any second chances in the storm that's coming our way.'

The hurricane reached them in the middle of the night. The wind howled around the *Almax Venturer* as if she were the sole target of its fury. The swell of the sea slowly increased. There was no way of avoiding the storm. The hurricane had them in its grip, like a giant fist gradually closing in.

The officers on the bridge were the first to realise the danger.

'How does it look, Mr Hill?' asked Captain Thomson, who had relieved the first mate at the wheel.

'There's no weather forecast for these latitudes,' said Mr Hill. 'Only a drift ice warning.'

'That's the least of our problems right now.' Captain Thomson leaned over the shimmering green radar screen. 'Not many clouds,' he said, 'but some curious areas there. Like flocks of birds. What d'you think, Mr Hill?'

Mr Hill bent over the screen. 'It's not unusual to see little so near the Pole,' he said.

'We're some nine hundred miles from the Pole, Mr Hill.'

'All the same,' the third mate said, 'there's no land between us and the South Pole, just water. That makes a difference.'

'Ships?' asked Captain Thomson.

'There are probably a few supply vessels on the move,' said Mr Hill. 'The pack ice will be closing in fast now. This is the last chance to get food and fuel to the Antarctic stations. In a month's time it'll all be frozen solid, and then no more ships will get through till next spring.'

'Have you made radio contact with any vessels?'

'No, though I'm listening to all frequencies. Too much static interference. There's a station transmitting somewhere – I'm receiving weak signals. Can't make anything out. It could be a base in the Antarctic, maybe the Russians. I'm not sure, but I have a kind of feeling they're not transmitting in English.'

'Naval craft?'

'Nothing. And if it's the Russians they won't be giving their position away.'

'Well then,' said Captain Thomson, 'we have to rely on our own resources. I have every confidence in you, gentlemen. And in the *Almax Venturer*,' he added, with a hint of a smile.

Peter lay awake all night. The waves kept on rising. The hurricane howled deafeningly, and the *Almax Venturer* groaned aloud as she flung herself into one mountainous wave after another. But although the elemental force of the sea made the fifty-thousand-ton vessel dance like a toy, she sprang no leaks. Her engines did not miss a single stroke.

In the first four hours, they lost the ship's boat and both derricks. There was nothing anyone could do about it. The sea had taken over the upper deck; sending a man out there would have been murder.

'She'll never stand it,' said Peter. He almost had to shout to make himself heard.

'Ships can stand more than you think,' said John.

'But the waves – they're so tall. They'll capsize us!'

'Fifty thousand tons don't capsize that easily. Take my word for it, so long as we're watertight we'll survive any storm. Ships only sink when they spring a leak.'

'How can you keep so calm? We ought to do something.'

John laughed. 'What do you suggest? We're stuck where we are – we might as well be on the moon. Anyway, they're doing all they can up on the bridge.'

'Why don't we turn? I mean, it's pointless running into these waves.'

'We can't turn. Not in a storm like this. Think what'd happen if the waves struck us broadside on!'

Before Peter could reply, a siren sounded somewhere inside the ship; a long note followed by several short ones.

'Fire!' cried John, rushing out of the cabin.

Sam met them in the corridor.

'Where is it?'

'No idea!'

They hurried to the assembly point near the exit. Len arrived, out of breath. 'It's in the engine room!' he called.

'Bad?'

'Don't know. Lot of smoke on the 'tweendeck.

Doesn't seem to have worked its way upwards.'

'Where's Taylor, dammit?'

The men ran to the exit hatch. The bulkhead door to the 'tweendeck was closed; Bruce and the bo'sun were waiting beside it.

'Where's the hoses?'

'Just coming. Sam, you and Bruce run a second hosepipe out. We have to get in here. The hatches to the upper deck are closed tight.' Sam and Bruce hurried off.

'Help me get this door open,' said the bo'sun.

The bulkhead door was made of massive steel. The flames could not be far away, for the men felt the heat as they leaned against the door and its metal gave slightly.

'Come on, all together!'

The men flung themselves against the door at the same moment. At the third attempt it burst open.

They were immediately enveloped in smoke.

'Close it!'

Coughing and fighting for breath, exerting all their strength, they closed the door again.

'Right, get the breathing apparatus – quick!'

Andy and the cook appeared with the first hosepipe. 'Open the door!' called Andy.

'Can't. Too much smoke.'

'Just a crack so's we can shove the hosepipe through.'

They pushed against the bulkhead door again. This time it gave way more easily.

Andy wedged the end of the pipe firmly between the door and the frame, then opened the valve, and water sprayed into the 'tweendeck at high pressure. Smoke kept billowing through the crack as thickly as ever.

Mr Beagles arrived at the same time as the second hosepipe.

'The first engineer's down there,' he said. 'They're still in contact with the bridge. How's it look here?'

The bo'sun pointed to the bulkhead door. 'Too much smoke. As soon as the breathing apparatus comes we'll try to get in. We need to get at the fire. Did Jack say where it's worst?'

'It's obviously burning on the 'tweendeck. He's cut off by the fire. He thinks it'll soon get down to him. All he has is a low-pressure hose and a few fire extinguishers – that won't do much good if burning oil or petrol gets into the engine room. There are several barrels of petrol, diesel and hydraulic oil on the 'tweendeck.'

Soon the men arrived with the breathing apparatus, and they hastily put it on. No job was easy in the heavy swell which snatched the floor away from under their feet and seemed to push the walls away.

They stumbled forward. Every second counted.

The 'tweendeck was open at the centre, like a vast swimming pool whose floor was the engine room. Narrow galleries ran around the walls, with gangways down to the engine room at intervals. At the level of the galleries there were several stowage areas where tools and fuel were stored.

Through the smoke, they saw the red glow of the fire.

'My God!' exclaimed Mr Beagles. 'What the devil's burning there?'

The whole wall ahead of them seemed to be engulfed in flames.

'Where does it . . . ' John began, and then saw where it came from. The crack was hardly a hand's breadth in size, but it ran half across the width of the ship. It was in the partition between themselves and the foreship – and the fifty thousand tons of crude oil carried there.

'One of the tanks is leaking,' said John. 'Oil must have got into the cavity.'

The men directed the jets of both hoses at the crack. Water is not a good method of fighting burning oil, but its sheer pressure will often be enough to cut off a fire's air supply.

'Stop!' called Mr Beagles.

All along the crack the fire was burning as fiercely as ever, with thick, black smoke that stifled the men even through their breathing apparatus. Even worse, however, the water from their hoses had washed burning oil along the wall and down into the engine room. The first engineer was running from side to side with an extinguisher, but it did not hold much foam and was soon empty.

Mr Beagles looked helplessly at the crack in the wall. He had plenty of experience with tankers, and knew their weak points, the places where tension cracks were most likely to occur. This was not one of them. It was the strongest place – it had to be, dividing the engine room from the oil tanks as it did. But the crack was there now, and every movement the ship made pushed more oil out of the tank.

'Run out as many hosepipes as possible,' ordered Beagles. 'Half up here, the other half down in the engine room. We'll have to risk it. The bilge pumps should deal with some of the water. Good luck,' he added, automatically. Deep down inside him, he knew it was hopeless. It was only a question of time before the fire reached the cavity. Perhaps the oil was already burning. Then it would not be long before one of the main tanks went up,' and nothing would be able to put such a fire out.

Very likely most of the men realised the situation. They worked with dogged determination, on and on, hour after hour. Everyone fought the fire, including the officers, who relieved one another at the wheel so that they could help out in the engine room.

Sometimes they seemed to be getting the better of the fire, but even when the flames were licking quite gently it only needed a small gust of wind to fan them up again, with a loud roar, until they were as fierce as ever.

The bilge pumps could not deal with so much of an additional workload. After two hours, the engine room was knee-deep in water.

'I'll have to stop the engines,' said the first engineer. 'The water's too high. We have to turn either the engines or the hoses off.'

Captain Thomson had no choice: he gave orders to stop the engines. As long as they were fighting the fire they still had a chance of saving the ship.

Without her engines, the *Almax Venturer* was helpless. She no longer responded to the wheel. The waves flung her bows sideways and drove her onward like a piece of flotsam.

They had been transmitting distress signals for three hours, but there was so much interference that they could not tell if anyone was receiving them.

It was almost impossible to stand upright now. The ship was rolling at over forty degrees. The men in the engine room lay on the floor and clung to the struts and footwalks as they tried to direct jets of water on the flames. The bo'sun was lying beside John MacGraw. They had both pushed up the masks of their breathing apparatus. The smoke was not so thick now, and the apparatus got in their way. Their faces were blackened with smoke, and John was bleeding from a long scratch on his forehead. They were both lying by the same hosepipe, trying to direct its nozzle upwards.

'No use!' gasped the bo'sun. 'She's rolling too hard. Why doesn't the old man turn her out of the wind, dammit?'

'He can't,' John pointed out.

The bo'sun smiled, a twisted smile. 'I've got the edge on you this time!' he said. 'Hey, Mr Beagles! Come here!' he called, before John could answer that one.

The first mate worked his way slowly over to them. 'What is it?'

'An idea,' said the bo'sun. 'How to bring her bows about.'

'How?'

'Use the anchors.'

Mr Beagles stared incredulously at him. 'Good God, Taylor! D'you know how deep the water is here? We'd only get them a fraction of the way down.'

The bo'sun shook his head vehemently. 'Doesn't matter,' he said. 'The anchors don't have to reach the bottom. Sea anchors, get it? The resistance they supply will be enough to swing the ship round.'

Mr Beagles thought about it for a moment. 'Are you sure?'

'Well, I can't guarantee anything. I only saw it done once, on a freighter. It worked then.'

'Maybe,' said Mr Beagles, 'but I don't see it working in this hurricane. Who'd operate the windlasses? Sending a man the whole length of the ship would be murder.'

66

The bo'sun looked at John. It was a duel neither man wanted to lose.

Suddenly the bo'sun smiled. 'I'll go,' he said, and before anyone could say a word he had got to his feet and was making for the bulkhead door, ducking low.

'Hang on, Taylor – I'll come with you.'

Mr Beagles held John back by his arm. 'We need every man we've got down here,' he said firmly. 'It's our only chance. Taylor will turn back when he sees the deck. Nobody could get through. Some of the breakers are over ten metres high.'

The bo'sun had reached the door to the upper deck. The ship was rolling so violently that waves washed over the glass pane. Taylor waited until the *Almax Venturer* righted herself, then undid the storm bolts and pushed the door open.

The hurricane instantly flung him back against the ship's superstructure. He found a handhold before great cascades of water crashed over him and down to the deck. He stood there motionless for an eternity, pressed against the wall. Then the ship righted herself again and he ran for it, away from the rail and towards the middle of the deck and the cluster of pipelines there. The *Almax Venturer* rolled to starboard, and the bo'sun almost flew right across the deck. Only the pipes brought him to a halt. A coupling struck his knee painfully, but the pain was not going to stop him now.

He waited, silently calculating the seconds during which the deck would be free before the ship heeled over again.

There was not much time, but enough to jump a few metres forward. The bo'sun fought for every metre's progress. Sometimes the breakers fell on him, and he held his breath until his lungs seemed about to burst. He never looked back, only forwards, to the bows and the capstan that he had to reach. He felt quite calm, fearing only that there would not be enough steam pressure from the boilers to operate the windlasses.

And then he had reached the bows, and the windlasses were slowly turning. The cables came rattling through the capstan, pulled by the weight of the sea anchors now, going faster and faster until their entire length was paid out. They hung far down into the sea like two gigantic fishhooks, and, sure enough, the ship slowly began to turn in the direction of the waves.

The bo'sun was on his way back. The *Almax Venturer* was not rolling so violently now that the waves no longer struck her broadside on. However, it was not easy for the bo'sun to get across the deck, and he often had to wait several minutes to summon up the strength to go the next few metres.

He was smiling contentedly. He had done it. All by himself.

He stopped again. The quarterdeck. He knew every inch of this ship. The engine room lay below him. He was now standing directly above the partition wall. He thought of John MacGraw lying somewhere there below. He had looked for fear in John's face before he went out himself. But John had not been afraid. He would have done just the same if Taylor had sent him out. In that, they were like each other.

That was the bo'sun's last thought. Beneath his feet, the thick steel plates of the deck exploded into a wall of fire that shot vertically to the sky. Bert Taylor was dead even before the sound of the explosion shook the *Almax Venturer*.

All hell was let loose in the engine room.

'Out!' shouted Mr Beagles. 'Everyone out!'

No one knew how much damage there was. They could only see the fire, and it was vast. They could do nothing to fight it with their few hoses.

The whole quarterdeck was engulfed in flames.

They assembled by the exit hatch. Only Taylor was missing.

'We can't wait any longer,' said Captain Thomson. 'Mr Beagles, get the lifeboats ready and divide the men between them. We have three boats. As soon as the first boat's manned, cast it off. I'll take the last boat with Mr Hill and Mr Brenagan. We've been transmitting emergency signals and details of our position all the time – no answer yet. It's not likely we can stick together in this storm. Just let yourselves drift. Conserve your strength. We're somewhere around fifty-two degrees south, seventy-four degrees east. I don't need to tell you that the nearest mainland is Antarctica. Over a thousand kilometres to the south. We've been driven far off course. Karpog is somewhere to our west. That's the place to make for, men. I take the responsibility for this. The company asked me to change course, but the decision was mine alone. I'll wish you the best of luck . . . and God be with you,' he nodded quietly.

Peter felt fear like a lump of ice in his chest. Only a few days ago he had been wondering what it would be like if the ship sank.

But she's still afloat, he wanted to shout, we're still safe.

However, he kept his mouth shut. No one else was shouting, no one lost his head. Most of the men had practised for such an emergency for years. They had rehearsed this brief moment again and again, until fear was replaced by routine.

'Stick close to me,' said John. 'We're to go in the first boat.'

7

The day began with bright sunshine in Cape Town.
Table Mountain glowed rich gold above the city and
the harbour. There was a clear view to the horizon.
Just like a picture postcard, with the usual conglom-
eration of ships outside the harbour entrance, waiting
for a place by the pier or in dock. Their numbers
never decreased. If one ship left another one came
in and got in line to wait.

All was noise and bustle on the dockside. Everywhere, ships were being loaded and unloaded. Countless cranes swung their arms over hatches and holds.
Choice woods, sacks, metal containers stacked in the
port like giant building blocks.

At the far end of the harbour, by the entrance to
the dry docks, lay the *Petite Mouette*. She carried the
name of her home port on her stern: Marseille. The
Petite Mouette was a tug with an ugly superstructure
set down on her deck like a square crate. The wheelhouse was on top, with cabins for a four-man crew
underneath. The tug sat low in the water, looking
like a vessel that could sail in any sea. She had two
water cannon fore and two aft, each of them able to
shoot a concentrated water-jet two hundred metres
into the air.

Under her bulging hull there were two Sulzer

71

diesel engines, each of which delivered six thousand horsepower to the propellers. She could do thirty knots and keep that speed up for hours on end. And she was strong enough to take any ship ever built in tow with one of her steel hawsers. She had five kilometres of hawser on her winches. She sailed under the French flag, but any captain worth his salt knew it for a flag of convenience. The *Petite Mouette* should, in fact, have sailed under the skull and crossbones. She was a pirate vessel of the modern variety, and she was only in Cape Town because she was waiting for prey.

Now that winter storms were raging around the Cape of Good Hope, the pirates descended on Cape Town. Germans, Swedes, Americans. They were all waiting for a ship to get into distress. Then they would put out and offer their help. For a fee. Their help did not come cheap. It often cost more than a ship's cargo. But the ships' captains had no choice: either they agreed to the salvage company's conditions, or they would lose both cargo and ship.

The *Petite Mouette* was registered as a salvage vessel, the property of the Roussolet salvage company. Anyone who looked into the matter, however, would soon have discovered that apart from the *Petite Mouette* the Roussolet salvage company had no property. Only debts to the bank. And something else would have come to light too: the company consisted of just one man, Julien Roussolet by name.

He was a heavily built man with the sea in his blood. He had a thick beard, in which his mouth was visible only when he laughed. Or shouted. At this moment he was shouting through the engine room hatch.

'Going to be much longer, Albert?'

72

'Nearly ready, skipper. We can put out after lunch.'

Julien growled angrily. 'What for? The rest of 'em will have snapped up all the best pickings by now.'

'Oh, there'll be something left for us, Julien. That was one hell of a storm.'

'And we sat it out in port with engine trouble!' bellowed Julien.

'Not my fault,' replied Albert.

'Okay, okay. I'm not blaming you personally. We need a commission. The bank keeps getting after me. If I don't have our finances in order by the end of the month the *Petite Mouette* will go under the hammer. Want to go back to your department store?'

Albert shrugged his shoulders. 'Can't be helped. Nothing you can do about it. Engines need servicing or they'll break down. That's the fact of the matter, so if you want a scapegoat you'd better pick on yourself.'

'Okay, Albert,' said Julien, soothingly. 'I know what you mean. It's just the frustration, see? All those missed opportunities. We'd have all our troubles behind us if only . . . '

'Shut up, both of you!' called Maurice Furnier. He was sitting bent over the radio equipment, turning knobs.

Julien listened. Maurice had turned up the volume to maximum. Loud crackling came from the loudspeaker.

'Just a lot of jumbled waves,' said Julien.

'Ssh!'

They listened, holding their breath.

'Can't hear a thing,' said Julien, after a while.

Maurice put both hands over his headset. 'It's very faint,' he said.

'What is, for God's sake?'

'Mayday. No doubt about it. It's a distress signal.'

'Where from?'

'Quiet . . . my God, it could be from the moon, it's so faint.' Maurice pointed to the tape recorder above their heads. 'Quick, switch it on.'

Julien lunged forward and pressed the Record button. Leaning over, he put his ear close to the loudspeaker.

'Here it comes again!'

This time Julien heard the faint voice, like a soft whisper. 'Abag Fent . . . ' he said at last. 'Or something like that.' Straightening up, he rummaged among files and maps until he found Lloyds' Register. He opened it and ran his finger up and down the columns.

'Here we are!' he cried suddenly. 'Holy Moses! Here's a turn-up for the books! The *Almax Venturer*. Tanker, fifty thousand tons. Our troubles are over, Maurice. Fifty thousand tons. Where is she, dammit?'

'Here we are again,' said Maurice. '*Almax Venturer* . . . yes, that's it. But her bearings are too faint for me to pick up. Where's she from?'

'Home port Sydney, Australia. Belongs to a firm called Almax.'

'Australia,' said Maurice thoughtfully. 'Where would they be? And not forgetting the main point – are they carrying a cargo of oil, or is the tanker empty?'

'A fifty-thousand-ton tanker never sails empty, Maurice. My God, suppose she's got a full cargo aboard! We could all retire. Or we could buy two new boats . . . '

'Keep your hair on, Julien. We don't know anything

74

yet. It would be a great help to have a rough idea of their course. Can you ask around?'

'We could telegraph Almax,' Albert suggested.

'No, they'd send their own boat out then. Nobody else must hear of this. In no circumstances, understand? The *Almax Venturer* is ours!'

'Okay, Julien,' said Maurice. 'All the same, I think you should ask around. Try the harbour authority and the supply companies. They're probably on their way to Europe. If they have to round the Cape they're sure to have ordered provisions and fuel somewhere.'

'Right. Stay right there by the receiver. We need a fix on their position.'

'I'll do some work on the tape,' said Maurice. 'If I re-record it often enough I can get rid of the high frequencies. With luck we'll have their position in an hour.'

Julien was back only half an hour later.

'Lady Luck's with us this time!' he said triumphantly. 'The *Almax Venturer*'s carrying fifty thousand tons of crude oil for the Helcheman refinery in Rotterdam. They've booked a supply ship, but obviously they've had to avoid a storm and they're late arriving. How's it going, Albert?'

'All clear, skipper.'

'Good. Then let's get moving.'

Julien started the diesel engines. Soon they were turning over nicely. Albert cast off. At the same moment Julien opened the throttle valve, and the *Petite Mouette* moved away from the pier with a contented purring sound. Then her engines roared, and she shot out of the harbour basin, leaving a foaming wake behind her.

Albert put his head into the wheelhouse. 'Which way?' he asked.

'South-east,' said Julien. 'She's somewhere between here and Australia.'

Albert laughed. 'Talk about a needle in a haystack!'

Maurice took his headset off. 'I've got the latitude pretty well certain,' he said. '52° 49′ 20″ south. I'm not so sure of the longitude. Probably somewhere around seventy degrees east. Seventy-something. I can't make out minutes and seconds.'

Julien went over to a big nautical chart on the back wall of the wheelhouse. 'What are they doing so far south? They've deviated almost twenty degrees from the usual route.'

Maurice shrugged his shoulders. 'Can anyone get there before us?'

'Not from Cape Town,' said Julien. 'Our friends are all busy.'

'How about Australia? They won't be sitting around twiddling their thumbs at the Almax offices.'

Julien measured the distance with the span between his thumb and little finger.

'Almost the same distance,' he said. 'As far as I know there's only the Dutch anywhere around in the South Pacific, and even if they've picked up the Mayday call they won't get there before us. The Australians have only two tugs that could do the job, and if my information's correct they're both otherwise occupied in South-East Asia.'

'Then the *Almax Venturer* really is ours,' said Maurice. 'Supposing she's still afloat,' he added, after a minute.

Julien Roussolet turned abruptly away and looked back at Cape Town. He did not want Maurice to see from his face that he felt a certain shame: this was the first time he had given a thought to the crew of the *Almax Venturer*.

8

Peter bit his hand hard. The pain shot through his arm like a red-hot iron, but his nausea was as bad as ever. Nothing did any good now. The sweetish smell of vomit seemed to have seeped into every pore. All that mattered was the next breath of air, which would bring the smell back.

On the other side of the lifeboat, Sam was retching in the throes of a fresh attack.

'My God, I wish he'd stop,' groaned Len. 'He'll be puking his heart up next.'

John leaned over Sam, raised his eyelids, and then laid a hand on his forehead. 'Feverish,' he said. 'He can't keep anything down. We'll have to force water into him. Every ten minutes or so, till the fever's not so bad.'

No one replied. They were too exhausted to speak, or to think of anything but their own troubles. Their clothes were wet, sodden as sponges, and with the wet came the cold that shook their bodies. And there was nothing they could do but wait.

They had lost all sense of time. It was only a night they had been adrift, but each second of that night had brought its own torments.

All Peter could remember was the flames. The whole sea had seemed to be burning. Then they had slipped down over the crest of the next wave, and the *Almax Venturer* had disappeared from sight. Later, he thought he had seen a faint glow in the distance, but he was not sure.

Their boat would hold twelve men. There were only six of them. The *Almax Venturer* had been carrying three inflatable rubber dinghies. They were much the safest kind of lifeboat yet developed, made of specially toughened rubber divided into several tubular sections. They were inflated by gas cartridges; later on they could be blown up with a pump, through valves. The base of the lifeboat was a circle, like a children's swimming pool, covered with a plastic dome. There were no windows, and they had closed the only opening with a double zip fastener. The whole lifeboat was bright yellow. The faint light of dawn shone weakly into the interior of the boat.

The men were huddled around the sides, trying to hold tight to the tubular sections, but every wave sent them hurtling helplessly about. They had lost count of the number of times the boat had capsized and they had righted it again by shifting their weight.

Pockets were let into the boat in three places. They held water, food and medicaments. John had taken command without being asked, and no one questioned his authority.

They had enough drinking water for two weeks, but even after that they need not die of thirst. For some time, tablets had been available to filter the salt out of sea water so that it would fall to the bottom of a container as a sediment. The treated water tasted bitter, but it was drinkable. They had two boxes of these tablets in the boat.

The storm slackened slightly on the second day, and they opened the zip fastener a little way.

As well as Sam, Bruce and Len now had attacks of fever and shivering.

'It's the wet,' said John. 'We'll have to dry our clothes, or it'll get to us all.'

They undressed and hung their clothes up as best they could in the domed roof of the boat. They were not much colder naked than they had been before, in their clothes. Peter made soup, using a fuel cartridge which lasted just long enough to warm up a litre of liquid.

One of the men was always on watch by the small opening in the yellow plastic dome. They hoped to see a plane or a ship, though no one really believed that would happen.

Sam died on the morning of the third day. No one knew just when. Early in the morning, he drank half a mug of tea, and the next time John bent over him he was dead.

John drew the hood of Sam's jacket over his face. No one dared look at the dead man, and when the boat rose on a particularly high wave, he rolled from one side of it to the other. They decided to bury Sam at sea.

They had nothing to wrap him in. The wind was so bitterly cold that they could only open the dome very briefly to let his body slip into the water. No one said anything. They avoided one another's eyes, as if they were all somehow guilty. Then Bruce swore, loud and freely, in another fit of fever.

Peter was crying openly.

'Our Father, who art in heaven . . . ' he began to pray, and unexpectedly the men joined in. One by one, even those who thought they had long ago forgotten the words.

'Here's to Sam!' said John. Each of them took a sip from the small bottle of rum, and they found they could talk to each other again.

The wind died down on the fifth day, and the waves grew calmer. They were able to keep the dome open for several hours. Their clothes were almost dry, and the bottom of the boat was clear of water. For the first time, they thought they actually might survive.

Bruce and Len were still feverish, but at least their condition seemed to be getting no worse.

'Let's hope it's not pneumonia,' John whispered to Peter. Peter's own attack of seasickness had passed off again, and Andy's arm, which he had hurt when the boat was launched, was all right now too.

They took turns doing their few daily tasks. Nursing Bruce and Len was the most time-consuming, and none of them really knew much about first aid or the use of the few medicaments they had found in the boat.

The dome, once opened, acted as a sail and drove them before the wind. They made good speed. John estimated their course as south-south-west, but he was not sure, since he could not take their bearings from the position of the sun.

He had checked their supplies. They had several flares and smoke bombs, as well as a small short-wave transmitter, which they did not use much because they were not sure how long its batteries would last. They switched it on for five minutes every half-hour.

'Do you think they'll send a plane?' asked Peter. It was his watch, and he was standing at the side of the boat so that he could see as far out as possible into the endless grey around them.

'Who?' said Andy.

'Almax,' said Peter. 'They must realise we're missing by now.'

'That's right.'

'You do think they have, don't you?'

'Sure, but it's not that simple. I'd be more inclined to expect help from one of the Antarctic bases. The Americans have several planes stationed in Antarctica. But it's a big area, and we abandoned ship five days ago.'

'All the same,' said Peter, 'I bet they find us tomorrow. The sun's almost breaking through again. They'll find us tomorrow.'

Suddenly he fell silent.

'What's that?'

'What?'

'There. On the horizon.'

'Can't see a thing.'

'I can. Come here and look along my arm.'

Andy scrambled up behind Peter on the uppermost tubular section of the boat and looked over his shoulder. 'You're right,' he said. 'There's something there. Probably an iceberg.'

'I reckon it's land.'

'You're nuts.'

'No, really. It's too big for an iceberg. I've got a kind of a feeling.'

'You and your feelings!'

John joined them. 'It's a fair size,' he agreed, after taking a long look.

They kept their eyes fixed on the horizon. The colour of the sea was changing very slightly.

'Not so deep here,' said John.

They saw more and more seabirds. Once a great flock flew over them, high in the sky. Peter felt sure they had not seen birds just like these before.

Then, suddenly, there was seaweed drifting in the water. Long, leathery straps of eelgrass that rocked on the waves like brown snakes. After a while Andy fished up a twig out of the water. It came from some kind of thorny bush. By now they were sure they were approaching land.

'What d'you think – is it the Antarctic?'

'Can't be. We could never have drifted that far in five days. It must be an island.'

Peter remembered the Captain's last words. 'Karpog?' he asked.

'No idea,' said John.

'Let's hope it's inhabited,' said Andy.

John laughed bitterly. 'By penguins, maybe.'

They had two wooden paddles on board, but if they went on drifting the way they were going they should reach land without any help. Soon they were close enough to make out details. The island was not very large. Andy estimated its length as fifteen kilometres. One side was flat and rocky, the other covered with ice. Several glaciers seemed to flow into one another, and at their centre a white peak rose some three thousand metres above sea level.

They began paddling now, to get to the flatter side. The rocks were white in places, as if covered with snow, but when they came closer they realised that the white patches were great flocks of seabirds sitting on their eggs.

'Hey, look at that, John!' exclaimed Andy in excitement. 'I see a house! Now what d'you say? Penguins never built a house, that's for sure!'

'Well, no,' John admitted. 'Though I wouldn't exactly call it a house.'

They could see it clearly now. It was a corrugated iron hut, with a chimney of the same metal on one side. The corrugated iron gleamed as if it were new.

'What can it be?'

'No idea,' grunted John. 'We'll soon find out. We have to get past that reef first.'

He pointed to the rocky reef that barred their way to land. The surf was thundering on the rocks, white and foaming, as if the water were going to explode on the reef before it flowed gently in to shore. The reef was four or five metres high in places. However, the greater part of it lay below the surface, and only the line of the surf breaking showed just where it was.

John studied the line of the surf closely. 'We won't be able to make any second attempt,' he said. 'The reef would tear this boat to shreds.' He pointed to a sharp pinnacle rising from the water like a sword. 'There could be a channel to let us through beside that rock. What d'you think, Andy?'

Andy scrutinised the place carefully. The waves were rolling past the tall rock without breaking. 'Right,' he said, 'let's paddle for the rock, or the surf will carry us too far past it.'

John and Andy paddled for all they were worth. Reluctantly, the boat obeyed them. 'Harder!' shouted Andy through the thunder of the surf.

They began to turn around like a top. Foam whirled around them as if the sea were boiling. The surf had taken over their boat. Nothing they could do was any use. The sea and the current were in command, and the course of the surf decided which way they went. They shot forward as if thrust on by a giant fist. White fountains of foam broke over the dome of the boat and ran in through the opening.

Then it was all over, as suddenly as it had begun. The surf spat them out again and carried them towards the beach.

Peter jumped out of the boat. The ground was rocky, and covered with smooth stones rubbing against each other with the movement of the sea.

Carefully, Peter pulled the boat up over the stones until it was just grounded. John and Andy climbed out too and pulled it farther up on land.

John glanced over at the hut. It was about five hundred metres from the beach, half hidden behind two large rocks.

'We'd better get Bruce and Len up there first.'

John and Andy helped the two men, while Peter stayed with the boat. 'We'll carry the boat up too,' said John, when they had Bruce and Len safe inside. 'There's a sheltered spot out of the wind behind the hut.'

They dragged the boat up the long slope to shelter. The ground was rocky, with grass and bushes growing only in a few hollows. They stowed the boat behind the hut.

'Looks as if it was built yesterday,' said Peter. 'See that metal! And the screws all shiny as new!'

Andy shook his head. 'It's at least ten years old, maybe even twenty or more. You can tell that better when you're inside. From the framework. They don't fit girders together like that any more, haven't for some time. But the cold preserves it all – nails don't rust, not at these temperatures. The wood inside's like new too.'

'Who on earth would build a hut in a place like this?' asked John.

Andy smiled. 'Not me,' he said, 'but look at the

blue stamp on the metal. Lysaght, it says. Must be Australian.'

'What's it for, though?'

Andy shrugged his shoulders. 'Who cares right now?' he said. 'All I want to do is get good and warm.'

The impression the hut gave from outside was deceptive. Inside, it was quite roomy, and they could make themselves comfortable. The fireplace was made of stones, and instead of a smoke outlet pipe there was a chimney made of corrugated iron.

Half the floor of the hut was bare rock, and the other half had wooden planks as floorboards.

There were only two windows, without any glass in them. They were both on the same wall, and as narrow as loopholes. They were covered with metal plates, so that very little light made its way into the hut.

John fetched the waterproof matches from the lifeboat, and soon afterwards the fire was flickering up – slowly, until the chimney began to draw better.

They helped Bruce and Len to get near the fire, and as the warmth spread they took their damp jackets off. Nothing mattered as much as warmth just now. They would have to make plans for everything: eating, sleeping, drinking. But not now. Nothing would have drawn them away from that fire except human voices. However, they heard no sound outside except the noise of the wind blowing unceasingly against the corrugated iron.

9

'Our troubles have only just begun,' said Andy. 'The island only means temporary safety – the really tough bit's yet to come.'

'Stop that, will you, you wet blanket!' said Len, from his sleeping place near the fire. 'We have food, water and a roof over our heads. What more do you want? All we have to do is wait for someone to pick up our distress call.'

'Maybe,' Andy agreed. 'But we can't be sure anyone will. What I say is, we ought to be prepared for the worst.'

'Can't *get* much worse, can it?' Len pointed out.

'Shut up. Suppose they call off the search before anyone picks up our signals? We might have to stay here months. Maybe even years.'

'Stop talking like that, dammit!'

'There's no point in kidding yourself, Len.'

'I'm in a bad enough way as it is. I can do without you looking on the gloomy side, okay? And how come you're such an expert on survival techniques all of a sudden?'

'If you weren't lying there sick, I'd sock you one!'

'Come on, then, try it! I could beat you in my sleep!'

'Stop it, both of you,' said John.

'No.' Andy was sticking to his guns. 'This is too important. I was in the Scouts for years. It's a basic principle, see? Assessing a situation correctly. That's the only way we'll survive.'

Len laughed mockingly. 'The Boy Scouts! Big deal!'

'Got anything better to offer?'

'Let's vote on it.'

'On what?'

'Whether we're going to be good little Scouts. I reckon we've got enough provisions for several weeks, so if we just conserve our strength we can sit and wait for rescue – and that's it!'

'Okay, let's vote,' said John.

'Wait a minute,' said Andy. 'We can't vote on every decision we make. If you vote for what I say, you'll have to trust me.'

'That makes sense. Who's for Andy being in command?'

Peter and John raised their hands at the same time.

'You're the boss, then, Andy. What do you suggest?'

'We need a proper plan, and we need to stick to it. If we start by assuming we won't be found for a long time, our main job is getting hold of what we need most to survive. Food, water, firewood. Water's no problem. I reckon the hut was built here because the rock forms a natural cistern. It'll be harder to find food, but not impossible. Those seabird colonies can probably keep us going. And we may find other sources of food if we explore this island. Looks to me as if firewood's going to be our biggest problem. Nothing much seems to grow here except bushes. I suggest we start by laying in a good supply. Thick pieces of driftwood would be ideal. They won't burn as fast as bushes.'

'Somebody will have to keep a lookout,' Len said. 'I could do that.'

'No, you're not strong enough yet,' said John. 'You and Bruce had better stay here for the time being – at least until you've shaken off your fever. I suggest Peter takes the first watch. We'll have to change over quite often. Nobody ought to be out in this wind for more than two or three hours at a time.'

'What do I have to do?' asked Peter.

'Nothing,' Andy told him. 'Just keep your eyes and ears open. John will show you how to set off the flares and smoke bombs. Later on, we can collect a supply of wood for a signal fire too. Call us if you see anything.'

They warmed themselves in front of the fire once again, and then set off in different directions. Andy took the flat area of land extending to the foot of the glaciers. John went along the beach, and Peter climbed slowly to the highest point of the rocky part of the island. It was only about two hundred metres above sea level, but high enough to give a good view of the area.

The beach was much the same on both sides: flat and stony. On the side opposite the hut, however, the surf was less turbulent, and came rolling ashore in regular, unbroken waves. Peter felt sure that they would be able to row their boat out through the surf that side.

The nearest seabird colony was about a kilometre from the place where he stood. The birds were clustered so closely together that they scarcely had room to settle. They were constantly coming and going, and the wind carried their loud cries all over the island.

Peter collected stones and chunks of rock and began building a circle around his lookout point, as

88

shelter from the wind, which was so cold that it cut his face like a knife and made his skin peel as if with sunburn.

It was hard work. Every stone seemed to weigh a hundredweight.

Peter crouched behind the start of his protective wall. The icy peak of the strange mountain seemed close enough to touch. It looked like a frozen volcano, with glaciers instead of rivers of lava. Peter counted six separate glaciers flowing down from the mountain and into the sea.

Above the peak, the wind whirled crystals of ice and snow through the air in a fine, white cloud.

He had been surfing with his friends on Bondi Beach only four weeks ago! Going to sea had been a mistake. It would have been even if nothing had gone wrong. A ship was a prison, and you couldn't escape from it. Any more than we can escape from this island, thought Peter, ice-cold tears running down his cheeks. It was as if he had bottled up his tears too long, and now all the troubles of his life had suddenly merged at once. For the first time since the fire he found he could feel grief for the others: for Taylor and Mr Beagles, and Sam. In his mind's eye he kept seeing Sam's body sinking into the grey sea. He shook his head angrily. He wouldn't give up. Never. While there's life there's hope . . . he said it out loud to himself, quietly, like a spell to conjure up rescue.

Andy relieved him. 'See anything?' he asked.

Peter shook his head.

'Just birds,' he said.

'I've been thinking,' said Andy. 'About the hut, I mean. I reckon it's got something to do with the birds. Those two narrow windows look right towards their colonies. That can't be chance. I guess someone came here to watch them. Scientists, maybe, from a university or some sort of research institute.'

'Do you think they'll come back?'

Andy shook his head. 'John's found several empty cans,' he said. 'They buried their rubbish under some stones. Some of the cans still have labels on – complete labels. John reckons they're at least twenty years old.' He patted Peter on the back encouragingly. 'Don't let it bother you. We might have been much worse off. Go and get warm in the hut. John's back there already. He saw plenty of driftwood about. We'll collect it all, so we can keep the fire going the whole time.'

Peter went back to the hut. John had filled some of the larger empty cans with water and put them in the glowing embers, so that they would always have hot water ready to make tea.

Len had taken over as cook. 'I'm feeling a lot better,' he said. 'I can do my bit.'

The tea was weak, hardly more than hot water, and sweetened with only half a teaspoon of sugar, but it was warming.

'I'll keep all the old tea-leaves and dry them,' said Len. 'That way we can use them several times.'

John shrugged his shoulders. 'I never liked tea much,' he said. 'I wouldn't mind some good thick soup, though.'

'We've only got five cubes of soup concentrate left,' said Len. 'They won't go far.'

John licked his lips. 'I've another idea,' he said. 'Chicken soup with eggs.'

'Chicken soup!'

'Well, seabird soup,' said John. 'You can pick them up off the ground, just like that. They're not scared. I've just been walking right through them, and they hardly moved from the spot. Some of them are sitting on eggs. We can just help ourselves.'

'Bring me the birds and you can have your soup,' said Len. 'And if you happen to find any grass or other plants about the place bring them back too. Some of them might be edible. We could do with herbs to flavour our food. My mum knew a whole lot about herbs – sometimes we'd be given a whole field full of 'em for a salad.'

'Go carefully with those birds,' said Bruce, with difficulty. He was still feverish and talking cost him an effort.

'What d'you mean, carefully?' asked Len.

'Well, so's you don't frighten them. Take birds from the edge of the colony and don't go chasing them. They're only tame because they don't see us as enemies. If we scare them they'll soon learn, and then you can forget about chicken soup.'

'Hey, I never knew you knew so much about birds,' said Len, impressed.

Bruce tried to laugh, but it turned to a cough.

When they had warmed themselves up, John and Peter started out. They walked along side by side in silence for a while. The wind was blowing in their faces, so that talking wasn't easy.

They were going along the ridge that ran all along the coast. From there, they could get a good view of any driftwood on the beach.

'Did you see anything?' John asked, when they stopped in a place sheltered from the wind.

'When?'

'When you were on watch.'

'No, nothing.'

'I don't mean a ship or a plane – here on the island.'

'Only birds,' said Peter. 'Doesn't seem to *be* anything else here.'

John shook his head thoughtfully. 'I'm not so sure,' he said at last.

'What d'you mean?'

'Well, I didn't mention it to the others,' said John. 'I'm not sure, you see, and I don't want to look silly.'

'You can tell me.'

John nodded. 'Two pairs of eyes are better than one,' he said. 'When I was going along the beach earlier, I saw smoke.'

'Where?'

John pointed to the other end of the island. 'Somewhere right over there. Beyond one of the glaciers, I guess. Only a small wisp of smoke, and the wind soon blew it away.'

'Are you sure?'

'No, that's what I said! That's why I asked you.'

'Well, *I* didn't see anything,' Peter repeated. 'It could have been something else. When I was on watch I did see a white cloud above the peak there, but it was only the wind blowing snow or ice crystals around. Maybe you saw something like that.'

'Maybe,' said John, 'but it looked a lot like smoke to me.'

'Surely there'd be other traces,' said Peter. 'On our part of the island.'

'Of course! Nobody would be idiot enough to live on the ice if he had any choice.'

'Want to go and look?'

'It's too far, and we're not kitted out for it,' replied John. 'Andy thinks we'd better not explore the whole island until Len and Bruce are on their feet again, and I reckon he's right.'

For the next few hours they worked hard. They found a number of large pieces of driftwood. Planks from wooden boats that might have been wrecked thousands of kilometres away; the anchoring roots of seaweed, hard as the hardest of wood; branches of trees worn white and smooth by the salt water.

They made several piles of driftwood and then carried them back to the hut, one by one.

There was not quite so much to carry on their last journey. 'Let's go a slightly longer way round,' said John. 'Through the bird colony.'

'Chicken soup?' asked Peter, laughing.

As they walked across the flatter ground they looked more closely at those places where plants grew. Several of the bushes had dark berries. The grass was thin and threadlike. Only moss seemed to grow in abundance.

'Len can go and look for himself,' muttered John. 'I'd rather starve than eat moss.'

They walked through the middle of the colony. The birds were not disturbed, and hardly looked up. Only a few of them were sitting on eggs. Most of the chicks had hatched out and were running hopefully after anything that moved.

A few of the birds did not move from the spot, and John and Peter had to walk round them. Even when they waved their arms to shoo the birds off, they made way only with reluctance.

John did not know what the birds were called. He could tell they were seabirds, of course, but they obviously belonged to several different species. They were all large, with a wing span of over a metre and dark, grey or speckled plumage. They had long, strong beaks. Those few birds still brooding were all sitting on single eggs.

93

It was impossible to estimate the size of the colony. There were probably well over a hundred thousand birds. Where they nested, the ground was covered with a thick, white layer of dried droppings. The birds did not build nests, but laid their eggs on the ground.

John and Peter reached the other end of the seabird colony. 'Look – the birds do seem to have enemies after all,' said John. For they saw large quantities of plucked feathers lying among the rocks.

John stirred the feathers with the toe of his boot. There were birds' heads, legs and guts lying among them. 'I wonder what sort of creature did that?' said John. He picked up a large stone. 'I don't like this, but we have to eat, don't we?'

John killed three birds. It was as easy as picking blackberries. He slung the dead birds over his shoulder. Each of them weighed over a kilo. Then they went back again almost the same way as they had come.

Peter suddenly stopped.

'What's up?'

Peter pushed several birds aside, bent down and picked up something black and shiny.

'A pistol!'

He turned the pistol over in his hands, examining it. The barrel was short and thick, with ribbing along the side. There was an empty magazine in the gun. Letters were stamped into the metal on the back of the handle.

'*Reichsmarine*,' Peter spelled out slowly. 'Hey – that's German!' He remembered some scraps of German from his childhood; his mother had been Austrian before emigrating to Australia. 'I think it means Imperial Navy.'

'*Reichsmarine*?' said John, surprised. 'Yes – but Germany doesn't call itself an Empire any more. That was in Hitler's time. This must date from the Second World War.'

'You think the Germans were here then?' asked Peter incredulously.

'No idea, son. The Germans were all over the place then. My God – suppose they actually did land here thirty or forty years ago! It's not impossible.'

'Maybe the pistol belonged to someone else. One of the bird watchers, for instance,' suggested Peter.

'Could be,' John admitted. 'But ornithologists don't usually go around with Second World War German navy pistols. Pity these stones can't speak!' he added.

Peter pushed a couple of birds aside with his foot.

'What are you doing?' John asked.

'I might find more,' said Peter.

'What for?' asked John. 'A pistol's the last thing we need. I mean, it doesn't matter who was here years ago, not now.'

'How about that smoke you saw?'

'I wish I'd never mentioned it,' snapped John. 'Sometimes you want to see something so much, you end up thinking you really do see it. There isn't any smoke, and there's no one else on this island. A Second World War pistol doesn't change that.'

The others agreed when they had had a good look at the pistol after John and Peter got back.

'Somebody was here,' said Andy, 'and somebody left again. I reckon it's kind of cheering. We want to do just that ourselves!'

They soon forgot the incident. But Peter looked at the pistol several more times before he finally stowed it away in his corner of the hut, along with some pretty shells he had found on the beach.

They worked hard over the next few days. Their woodpile grew daily, and soon it was stacked high enough to cover two sides of the hut. Len was strong enough to give a hand now. He saw to preparing food. At first their meals consisted almost entirely of seabirds. The small stock of provisions they had found in the lifeboat had gone down rapidly, and they wanted to keep a little of it back as iron rations.

Roasted, the birds tasted very good, and the men never felt hungry. Yet their general health was gradually deteriorating. It showed in small things. They had to stop and rest more often. Sometimes they were exhausted even in the morning, and it was as much as they could do to get up.

Then the first ulcers broke out. Quite suddenly, and sparing none of them. Their skin turned dark in places, and then suddenly split into open sores.

'Vitamin deficiency,' said Andy. 'If we don't eat some kind of greens soon our teeth will fall out.'

John shuddered. 'Grass and moss – yuk!'

But Len solved the problem surprisingly quickly. He gathered large amounts of mosses and grass, berries, leaves and lichens. Then he began tasting them in small quantities.

'My God!' groaned John. 'You'll kill yourself with that stuff.'

'Got any better ideas?' asked Len.

There was no alternative, of course, and as time went by Len became bolder and more expert. He pounded the edible leaves, grasses and moss into a mush which they ate either raw or cooked like spinach.

Even John could not object to that, and the results showed within a few days: their sores soon healed.

Bruce was sometimes able to get up for an hour or so now, but he was still weak and needed nursing.

They made the hut as comfortable as possible. They built a table beside the fireplace, with a pedestal made of stones and a surface cobbled together out of planks of driftwood. Their chairs were made of rocks, upholstered with seabirds' wing feathers woven together. They cushioned their sleeping places with feathers as well to make soft, warm beds.

What they missed most was fabric or any other kind of material they could have made into blankets. Len experimented with sections of bark, trying to weave them together into a larger piece, but his first efforts were not very successful.

In time, they all worked out their own routines for getting through the daily tasks. There was ice to be hacked for drinking water, there were plants, berries, roots and wood to be collected, birds to be killed and plucked, and someone had to stay on watch and search the beach for anything that was washed up. This last activity produced some unexpected finds: bits of cork from buoys, ropes and lines, several plastic bottles and containers. There had been a fishing line and hook in the lifeboat, but it was no good trying to use it to fish from the beach. So John made a trap and put it out in the shallows of the calmer beach on the other side of the island. Sometimes he caught ten fish in a day, and what they could not eat fresh they hung up to dry in the air.

Andy kept insisting that they must stock up with provisions. He even planned to make a kind of larder in one of the glaciers. The weather was slowly changing. In the morning, the water was frozen in the natural cisterns, and soon it only ever melted on the surface. The wind was still blowing hard, day and night, never slackening for a moment. Once it snowed. But the flakes did not settle on the ground; the wind blew them all away.

The sun broke through less and less frequently. Usually the sky was a pale grey, almost white.

They called it 'The Expedition'. They often discussed it, but somehow or other there was always some reason to put it off. By now they knew their own part of the island quite well. But as they had seen from the boat, it was only a small part of the whole area. None of them expected the island to be inhabited, but there might be another headland beyond the glaciers and the snow-covered mountain, a headland with vegetation and birds. Perhaps even seals or other creatures.

They decided to go all round the island, in two groups. John and Peter would take the northern end, Andy and Len the southern end. John estimated that they ought to meet each other after five or six hours. Both groups had provisions with them, and each took a flare which they would fire off only if they were in trouble.

They set off early on the morning of the sixth day. John looked closely at the sky. 'Same old white mist,' he said. 'I wonder when we'll see the sun again?'

'It can't go on like this for ever,' said Peter.

'Who says? I don't know what it's like here in winter. Not too pleasant, you can bet.'

They went along the beach until they reached the foot of the first glacier. The surface of the ice was rough, criss-crossed with countless lines which gave a good foothold. They had to climb up the length of the glacier until a vertical wall barred their way.

They looked around. The sea lay about a hundred metres below. The waves broke directly on the ice here, with such violence that the ground shook. John pointed west.

'Doesn't look too good,' he said.

A second tongue of the glacier ran parallel to the first, and there was a deep crevasse between them. Shuddering, Peter looked down into the chasm below. The waves rolled right up to the far end of the glacier. Polished smooth by the water, the ice gleamed shiny green and blue.

'We'll never get across that,' said Peter.

John nodded gloomily.

'Why don't we try going over the mountain?' Peter asked. 'If we climb high enough we can skirt the glacier.'

John shook his head. 'We're not equipped for it,' he said. 'No rope, no proper climbing boots. Not even gloves, and I'm not risking my hands.'

'Then we'll have to turn back.'

'That's what it looks like.'

They searched the glacier for another way across, but it was no use. They would never get around the island this way.

'Maybe Andy and Len will have better luck,' said John, on their way back. 'The southern side doesn't look half as rugged. If they get stuck too we'll have to try it in the boat.'

They did not go the same way back. John wanted to take a closer look at the foot of the mountain. Up to a height of about eight hundred metres it was not covered by ice. It was not particularly steep here, and there were a great many rocks scattered about the place, which gave them a good enough foothold. These rocks were black and porous, a sure sign that ages ago they had flowed from the mountain in the form of lava.

They stopped where the ice began. Peter screwed up his eyes as he looked to the peak of the mountain. The brightness of the ice was dazzling. The sky was just the same colour as the mountain, and for a moment mountain and sky seemed to blend.

John looked back at the rocky part of the island. Their hut was out of sight, but a thin plume of smoke showed them roughly where it lay.

'I saw it again,' said John.

Peter turned in surprise. 'What?'

'Smoke.'

'Where?'

'Here,' said John slowly. 'Right here.'

'That's why you wanted to come up the mountain?'

John nodded. 'God knows what it is,' he said furiously. 'But I was dead sure of it this time. I did see smoke, I swear I did! And the smoke was coming from this very spot.'

Peter looked round, baffled. 'I don't see anything now,' he said.

'Of course you don't see anything now!' said John, still angry with himself. 'I guess I'm going slowly crazy. Or maybe it's my eyes playing tricks. Or something in the light.'

They climbed back down the slope in silence. On their way back they went down to the beach, where John had left several large pieces of driftwood. They carried the wood to the hut and added it to the stack of fuel by the back wall. Their hands were cold and numb, and they were glad they could get inside now, out of the wind.

When they opened the door they realised something was wrong at once; it was usually warm in the hut.

100

But now the fire had almost burned out. Their eyes gradually got used to the dim light.

Bruce had gone.

John swore out loud. 'The stupid fool!' he said angrily. 'He's much too weak to be walking around outside.'

'John!' cried Peter. 'The food crate. It's empty. He's taken everything with him!'

John whirled around and strode over to the corner where they had put the lifeboat after deflating and folding it.

'And the boat's gone! He's taken that too.'

'And the flares,' said Peter, 'and the emergency transmitter.'

John was cursing uninterruptedly. 'I'll wring his neck!' he promised. 'The stupid idiot! What did he think he was doing? He won't get far on his own, not in his condition. Damn, damn, damn! And when we'd been nursing him too!'

'He can't have gone far yet,' said Peter. 'Not with all that stuff. And he'll have to blow the boat up with the foot pump. He won't do that in a hurry.'

'You're right,' said John. 'Come on, we might catch up with him yet. He must have gone over to the other side of the island. He couldn't possibly have launched the boat this side.'

They raced off, through the middle of the nesting birds. They were panting, their lungs aching as they gasped for air. Only when they had reached the beach on the opposite side of the island did they stop.

'Nothing to be seen!' gasped John.

Peter rested his hands on his knees and fought off his rising nausea.

'Well, now what?' said John, at a loss. 'He can't have vanished into thin air.'

'Maybe he's hiding on the island,' said Peter.

John laughed, without humour. 'He wouldn't need the boat for that!'

'Unless he's waiting for a better opportunity,' said Peter, angrily. 'Can *you* think of any other explanation?'

'Okay, okay,' said John. 'Sorry, it's just my nerves. Dammit, I still can't grasp it. He must be right out of his mind, that's the only explanation. Fever, see? He might as well have committed suicide!'

Peter shielded his eyes with one hand. 'Here come Andy and Len,' he said. 'Maybe they've seen Bruce.'

'We couldn't get round either,' Andy called.

John was waving to them frantically. 'Bruce has disappeared. Taking the boat, and our provisions.'

When they had told Andy and Len what the position was, they all began searching the island. No one felt very hopeful of finding Bruce. If he really wanted to hide on the island there were so many possible places that they could only stumble upon him by chance. Secretly, they all felt sure he had set out in the boat.

'And we'll never know what the devil was driving him,' said John.

10

Realisation of the extent of their loss came only gradually. While they were prepared to accept Bruce's fever as an excuse, they couldn't forgive him for stealing the emergency transmitter. That transmitter had been their only hope of rescue, and now it was gone their fate seemed sealed. None of them really believed a ship would pass the island. Although they wouldn't admit it, privately they were beginning to adjust to the idea that they might be stranded here for ever.

However, they did not give up keeping watch. They built a large bonfire of dry wood by the lookout point, protecting it from the wind with a stone wall.

They relieved each other every two hours. John was on watch this morning. The others were sitting in the hut getting warm.

'Maybe we could build a raft,' said Andy. He was sure they would find the conditions were better on the other side of the island, where the mountain provided shelter from the wind.

'What with?' asked Ben.

'Driftwood. We've found several pieces of cork and a metal container. We'd collect enough material in time.'

Len laughed drily. 'At our present rate it'd take ten years.'

Andy lost his temper. 'I've had about enough of your snide remarks,' he snapped. 'You haven't found a single constructive thing to say since we landed on this damn island.'

'Well, so who set up as the survival expert? If you'd listened to me the boat would still be here. And the transmitter. But you had to go on your precious expedition. Don't you talk to me about snide remarks! It's the last time I ever listen to you.'

'Oh, stop it, for goodness' sake!' cried Peter. 'You've been sniping at each other the whole time these last two days. That's not going to make things any better.'

'Shut your trap!' hissed Len, and he marched furiously out of the hut.

Andy shrugged his shoulders and put another piece of wood on the fire.

'It's this island getting us down,' he said. 'Sometimes I feel I could scream. Last time I was on watch I cried like a baby, but it didn't help any. My ma always used to say you ought to let your tears out. She thought if you didn't they'd collect somewhere inside you and burst through all of a sudden.'

'Do you think they've given up looking for us?' asked Peter. He had to talk about it, even though they usually avoided the subject.

Andy nodded. 'No point in kidding ourselves. One week, maybe two, but then they'd give up. Can't blame them, can you? Our chances of survival were minute after the first few days, and they need their planes and ships for other jobs. No, so far as they're concerned we're dead.'

'But they can't just write us off!' said Peter.

'And the ship too. A tanker with fifty thousand tons of oil.'

Andy laughed harshly. 'You don't know how right you are! If the *Almax Venturer* was still afloat there'd be any number of ships and planes around the place. Afloat, she'd be worth a hundred million. The ship, not the crew, get it? Nobody's bothering that much about us, and the *Almax Venturer*'s worth nothing at the bottom of the sea. I guess Almax have already pocketed the insurance money.'

Peter shook his head. 'I don't believe they'd be so heartless,' he said.

Andy slammed his fist angrily into the wall. 'Why do you think we went so far south? Yeah, I know – to avoid the storm. Sounds good, right? Back in Sydney I'll bet they're saying they only lost the ship because they didn't want to risk our lives. Hill and Beagles were talking about it. They didn't know I could hear them. Almax wanted the old man to change course, and he did what they said. That's how it really was. We're here because Almax was going to make several million more on the deal if we took the southerly route. And I'll bet you Almax won't lose out in the end either. No, they'll have written the ship off long ago. And us with her.'

Peter knew Andy was right. But at the same time he knew he would never give up hope himself. Hope was their one comfort. Hope meant life.

'Look, I'll get the birds if you like,' said Andy. He knew Peter hated that job.

'Thanks a lot. I guess Len's down on the beach. I'll give him a hand.'

They left the hut together. As usual, their first glance was at the sky.

The flare shot vertically upwards, with a thick

tail of red smoke, then reached the highest point of its flight and exploded with a loud bang that set off another cloud of red dust.

'John,' shouted Peter.

Len came running up from the beach. 'What's happened?'

'No idea. John must have seen something.'

They started to run. John's excited cries reached them from the lookout point.

'What's up, John?'

'A ship!' came the answer, like a shout of triumph.

'You sure?'

'Come here and see for yourselves!'

They all hurried up to the lookout point.

'There!'

And they all saw the ship. A tug with a clumsy superstructure amidships.

'Quick!' cried Peter. 'Light the bonfire!'

John was getting out the matches. 'Think I ought to fire the second flare off too?' he asked, as the first flames licked their hesitant way upwards.

'No,' said Andy. 'It's the only one we have left.'

But Len went round behind the wall of the lookout point and came back next minute with the second flare. 'Out of my way!' he told Andy grimly. 'You can't stop me. I'm going to send this flare up whether you like it or not.'

Andy moved as if to prevent him, then shrugged his shoulders and turned away.

'Len's right, Andy,' said John. 'My God, don't you realise? We're saved. They're bound to see us.'

The second flare hissed up towards the sky.

'Why don't they show they've seen us?' asked Len, after a while. 'Damn it, are they blind?'

Peter began shouting at the top of his voice.

'Come this way!' yelled John. 'We're here! Here!'
And he jumped up in the air, swinging both arms
above his head.

Len threw earth on the fire to make more smoke.
The tug remained on course – and then, suddenly,
disappeared.

'Gone,' said John, baffled. 'As if the sea had
swallowed it up.'

Peter was weeping openly, and was not ashamed to
let the others see his tears. 'Why?' he sobbed. 'Why
didn't they see us?'

Andy laid a hand on Peter's shoulder. 'They
couldn't see us,' he said quietly. 'There wasn't any
ship there.'

Though he spoke softly, John heard him and
whirled around. 'What d'you mean?' he shouted
angrily. 'We all saw it.'

Andy nodded. 'I saw it too,' he admitted. 'But
where was it?'

'Are you crazy?' cried Len. 'There was a tug out
there, and now it's gone. For God's sake, that's bad
enough – you don't need to rub our noses in it.'

Andy pointed. 'There's no water there,' he said
slowly. 'We're facing that damn mountain.'

They all stared at him for a moment, speechless.
Len was the first to pull himself together. 'Okay, so
we made a mistake,' he said. 'It was rather farther
out than we thought, that's all.'

Andy shook his head. 'No,' he said. 'We saw the
tug projected on the side of the mountain. It was a
mirage, get it?'

John swore. 'Like the smoke,' he said.

Andy nodded. 'It's something to do with the
sky,' he said. 'A friend of mine was once on a
supply ship in the Antarctic. When the sky and the

land were the same colour, he said, you could see the weirdest things. He swore he saw men and machinery the wrong way round. Like a mirror image, and upside down. And once he went a few metres from their camp and when he turned round it wasn't there. Gone. Dissolved into thin air. I don't know how it happens. Something to do with the light and the way it falls. The ship was a mirage.'

Len shook his head disbelievingly. 'You're not going to tell us the light could project a picture of a tug on the mountainside.'

'Yes, I am,' said Andy. 'The reflection of a *real* tug, see? A tug that could be God knows how far away from us.'

'But if the tug really exists it must be somewhere quite close.'

'Could be,' Andy admitted. 'But it might just as well be five hundred kilometres off. Don't kid yourselves. Nobody saw us.'

The incident depressed them all, but John took it worst. Somehow he seemed to feel he was wholly responsible for what had happened, and it got to the point where he wouldn't go on watch any more.

'We all saw it,' said Andy. 'It's not your fault.'

'I was the only one who saw the smoke,' John pointed out.

'So what? Conditions must have happened to be right for it while you were on watch, that's all. Listen, I know you don't mean to wriggle out of doing your bit, but we really do need everyone.'

In the end John took his turn on watch, but he was convinced he could no longer trust his own eyes.

'I don't look at that mountain any more,' he told Peter when they changed places. 'I'm scared to,

108

understand? This is the beginning of the end. We're all going crazy.'

'Oh, come on!' said Peter, crossly. 'Not unless we give up, we aren't. You've changed since we were on the ship.'

John laughed drily. 'Circumstances have changed, sonny. I was practically born on shipboard. I don't feel too good on land, and that's a fact. Takes me a while to get used to my surroundings when I'm on shore-leave. Even takes me a while to get used to my wife, and by the time I've adjusted I have to go back on board.'

'I never want to go on board a ship again,' said Peter.

John gave him an encouraging thump in the chest. 'You'll be okay, son,' he said.

Peter leaned against the wall of the lookout point, gazing out to sea. Even the water had taken on the milky white of the sky. Where the horizon usually curved against it there was no line now, as if sea and sky had merged into infinity. And their island was in the middle of it all, like a grain of dust, the solitary centre of the world.

Peter shook his head angrily. It was getting harder and harder to keep despair at bay.

He moved over to one side so that he could watch the beach in front of the hut. The surf ran regularly in against the reef. The waves followed a rhythm that changed with the tides. Just now it was seven little waves and then two big ones. One, two, three . . . he counted them. It helped kill time. His watch had stopped two days ago, or was it three? He didn't know why he hadn't wound it up. Every movement was an effort, and so was every thought.

How much longer till Len relieved him?

He could smell his own body. Like rancid butter. He hated the smell. This evening he would get undressed and wash all over. Plans, plans . . . he would end up just lying down like the others and sleeping a dreamless sleep until first light.

He let his mind wander. He thought of the most impossible things. A glass of Coca Cola, a hamburger. The pictures were so clear he could taste them.

They had all talked about it, over and over again. What they'd do first when they were rescued.

Peter scanned the sea. It was an automatic reaction. There was nothing to be seen that he hadn't seen a hundred times before.

He thought of Sam again, and was slightly ashamed. He knew it wasn't really Sam he was thinking of, but death. It wasn't that he was afraid of dying too. But not on this island, thought Peter, and then he saw the man.

No ship. No boat. Nothing. Just a solitary man in a white snowsuit with the hood up.

The man was walking cautiously along the sloping beach opposite, bending low like an animal scenting danger.

He did not look up at Peter; his attention was bent on the hut. Then Peter saw the gun. A rifle with a brown wooden butt.

It was not a mirage. Peter did not doubt the reality of what he was seeing for a moment. He heard a long-drawn-out shout that made the man on the beach swing round. Only then did Peter realise that he himself had shouted.

'Andy! John!' He never took his eyes off the man. From the hut, he heard the men's voices. 'Come here, quick!'

110

Suddenly the man ducked down, his body horizontal, the rifle pointing in front of him like a spear. Peter was aware of a shadow to one side of the lookout point. Len ran past him, keeping low. He must have seen the man, too.

'Careful. He's got a gun.'

Len glanced around without stopping. He nodded and put a finger to his lips.

Peter looked back at the spot where the man had disappeared. The slope of the opposite beach was not very steep, but a man could hide beyond it easily enough. Peter narrowed his eyes. Nothing to be seen.

Len was a third of the way over the level ground now. He was a good runner.

'What's up?' Andy and John clambered over the stone wall of the lookout point. 'What's up?' John repeated.

'A man,' said Peter. 'With a gun. Over there. Len saw him too.'

Andy and John looked incredulously at each other.

'What sort of a man?' asked John, finally.

'No idea,' said Peter, and then he suddenly remembered the way the man had moved and knew why it had struck him as familiar. 'A soldier,' he said.

'A soldier?'

'He ducked for cover,' said Peter. 'Like in war films.'

Andy shook his head in disbelief. 'Was he wearing uniform?'

'I don't know. Maybe it was uniform. Looked more like a protective snowsuit. White, I think. And boots.'

'I'll take a look,' said John firmly, and before Peter could say any more he had jumped over the wall and was running down the slope. Andy followed him.

'You stay there,' he called back to Peter. 'And if you see him shout as loud as you can.'

Peter shielded his eyes with both hands and stared at the top of the slope. There was no sign of the man.

By now Len had crossed more than half the level ground. He was making straight for the spot where Peter had first seen the man. He was not bothering to bend low anymore, but leaping over stones and bushes, taking long strides and swinging his arms to balance himself, like a gymnast doing floor exercises on the mat. Then, suddenly, he seemed to freeze in mid-stride. His arms went up into the air, and then down again as his whole body crashed to the ground.

Only then did Peter hear the sound of the shot.

Andy and John ran on until they reached Len. They dropped to the ground beside him. Len was half sitting up now. John supported him.

'See anything?' Andy shouted back to Peter as loud as he could.

'No.'

'Know where the shot came from?'

'No.'

Andy turned round again. 'Come down here,' he called after a while. 'Len's hit in the leg.'

Cautiously, Peter scrambled down to the level ground. Every few paces he stopped briefly to search the slope opposite with his eyes. It was when he reached the rocks where the level ground began that he saw the man again. He was hardly more than a shadow, a pale mark that showed briefly above the top of the slope, five or six metres from the spot where Peter had first seen him.

'There!' cried Peter. 'He's running away.'

Andy jumped up at once and gave chase. He was not a particularly good runner, and flailed his arms about like the sails of a windmill to keep his balance. Peter watched until he had disappeared beyond the slope. He held his breath until his lungs hurt. But the shot he expected to hear did not come.

Peter crouched down beside John, who had pushed up the leg of Len's trousers. 'Looks worse than it is,' he said. 'The bullet passed through. It hit the muscle, that's why there's so much blood. Run to the hut and get those bits of rag you found on the beach. And some straps of eelgrass, and a piece of string. We'll have to bandage it up good and tight or he'll lose too much blood.'

Peter ran back to the hut. When he returned with the bandaging materials, Andy was back again, too.

'No luck,' said Andy, still breathless. 'But I saw him. He ran along the beach to where the ice starts. That's where I lost him. There must be some way through.'

John nodded. 'We'll find him,' he said. 'As soon as Len's on his feet again.'

Len laughed, painfully.

'Does it hurt?' asked Peter.

'It's okay. At least I know it wasn't a mirage this time, that's for sure. What did he look like, Andy?'

'I didn't get a very clear view of him,' Andy admitted. 'He was much faster than me. All the same, I got the feeling he's not a young man. Can't quite say why.'

John looked up. 'Was he a soldier, Andy?'

Len cackled with laughter.

'A soldier! For God's sake, this isn't a joke!'

113

'Peter thinks the man was a soldier,' John explained. 'What do you think, Andy?'

Andy shook his head vigorously. 'Crazy!' he exclaimed. 'If I hadn't seen the blood I'd have thought we were all off our heads. Okay, so it did look like some kind of uniform outfit, and the gun was real enough too, right? But why the hell would he shoot at us? Even if he is a soldier. Good heavens, the nearest place where anyone's at war must be ten thousand kilometres from here!'

'I don't know why,' said John grimly, 'but we're going to find out, you bet your life!'

11

Peter shifted his weight from one foot to the other.
The cold was gradually intensifying. The dawn twilight
slowly gave way to daylight, which was not really
much brighter.

He wished today would turn out better than its
predecessors – better than every day since he first
talked to Ben Lexon about the job on the *Almax
Venturer*. He knew it did no good, but these days
he thought of almost nothing but the past and all
the things he would have done differently if he
could.

Len had been lucky. The bullet had done very
little damage to the tissues of the leg, and once they
had splinted it with two pieces of wood he could walk
unaided.

His wound had almost completely healed up in just
two days. It was almost a miracle. Andy thought the
eelgrass had helped.

They had searched every inch of the beach, but
no tracks showed on the rocky ground.

'He must have come from the other side of the
island,' John had said.

'But there's no way through,' Andy objected.
'The foot of the glacier cuts it right off.'

They searched the glacier again, investigating every

115

niche in the ice, every crack, every hollow, but still they could find no way through it.

'There's only one explanation,' said Andy at last. 'He came by boat. The glacier sticks right out into the sea like a wedge. It would be easy enough to round it in a boat.'

The others agreed. 'Next time he won't surprise us. Next time we'll surprise him.'

After that they kept the beach under constant watch. They found a crevasse in the ice deep enough to hold them all. At first they kept watch two by two, but there were not enough of them to keep a proper shift system going. If they kept watch individually they could shorten the shifts and have longer breaks.

'What do we do when he actually does turn up?' asked Len. 'He has a gun, and we don't.'

'We do nothing,' said Andy. 'All we need is his boat. Then his retreat's cut off.'

'And then?'

Andy shrugged his shoulders. 'We'll see. Good God, surely he won't shoot at us if we speak to him! Perhaps he really is a soldier and he thinks the war's not over yet. Last year they found two Japanese on some South Sea island who thought the war was still on.'

'He didn't look like a Japanese,' objected Len.

'Doesn't matter what he is, does it?' said Andy angrily. 'He's here now, anyway, and if we don't stop him he's liable to shoot us down one by one.'

This was another conversation that ended in a quarrel. Sometimes it took just one word or a gesture to set their tempers blazing. Their nerves were worn to a thread, and anger lay just beneath the surface like an ulcer that might erupt at the least touch. They were constantly shouting at each other for no

116

real reason, and when they finally stopped they had quite forgotten what started them off.

Peter ran his tongue over his lips. The skin was cracked, and the slightest touch was painful. The others had the same problem. All the same, Peter felt as if he were the only one suffering.

He beat his arms against his body and hopped up and down. How much longer till he was relieved?

The wind did not get into the crevasse in the ice, and if Peter went right to the far end he was in complete silence.

There was a green shimmer to the ice, even at night, which was hard to distinguish from twilight now.

'One man went to mow, went to mow a meadow . . . ' Peter laughed. He hadn't noticed he was singing out loud. Sometimes he found he was talking to himself too. It helped to stave off the loneliness. And the fear.

He had often wondered what he would do if he came face to face with the man with the gun. He wasn't really afraid of that moment. At least it would bring things to a head, mark a turning point in their slow slide into hopelessness and the ultimate fear.

Yet when it happened it was not at all the way he had expected. There was no warning, no time for preparation. He had heard nothing. The man was suddenly there, standing at the entrance to the crevasse in the ice, and the barrel of his gun was almost touching Peter's chest.

Peter could not feel anything. The surprise was too great, and as he stared fixedly back at the figure opposite, realisation came to him. The man was crazy. His eyes were the eyes of a madman.

He was a soldier, yes. No doubt about it. His

117

white snowsuit was thin, and full of holes through which the dark fabric of a military uniform showed. It was torn over his chest and held together with a large iron brooch shaped like an eagle, with a swastika below it held in the eagle's claws.

'English?' asked the man, in German.

Peter searched his memory. Although his Austrian-born mother used to speak German to her children when they were little, he had forgotten most of what he once knew. He shook his head.

'Got a cigarette?' asked the man, again in German.

Peter still said nothing.

'Come on, boy! Cigarette! Cigarette!' repeated the man, miming the act of smoking.

'No,' said Peter. He was still staring at the swastika on the man's chest. 'German?' he asked.

'What?'

Peter simply could not remember the German word for it. All he could think of were the war films he had seen on TV. '*Heil Hitler*,' he said.

The man's eyes narrowed. 'The hell with Hitler!' he yelled angrily, and then burst into wild laughter. 'Where's your ship, boy?' he asked, when he had calmed down.

Peter shook his head.

'Your ship!' repeated the man. 'Ship, dammit!'

Peter nodded. 'The *Almax Venturer*,' he said. 'An oil tanker. She sank.'

'What? Speak German, can't you?'

'She's sunk . . . *versunken*,' said Peter, slowly.

The man roared with laughter. 'Sunk, is she? Torpedoed. By a U-boat, eh?'

Peter was not sure if he had understood what the man was saying. 'The war is over,' he said, slowly.

'What?'

'War – er . . . *Krieg. Krieg kaput*,' said Peter. He couldn't remember the German for 'peace'.

The man laughed louder than ever. The barrel of his gun rose and fell with each new peal of laughter, but he never took his finger off the trigger.

'You don't know how right you are!' he said at last, and suddenly the expression on his face changed. He jerked his gun towards the entry to the crevasse. 'Come with me.'

'What?' said Peter, in English.

'Come with me!' repeated the man harshly.

Peter moved slowly sideways.

'And no tricks, or you'll get shot like your friend!'

Peter did not understand this bit, but he knew he was being told to go with the man.

The way into the crevasse was narrow, and Peter had to press close to the ice to get past the German. For a moment, they touched, and the man hastily pushed him on. It was the briefest of movements, but all the same Peter was surprised to feel the strength in the man's arm.

'Where to?' he asked. But the man seemed to have lost interest in talking to him, and simply pointed wordlessly to the beach.

The mouth of the gun was still directed at Peter's back. He tried to move as slowly as possible. Every second was valuable, but the barrel of the gun pushed him roughly forward.

They had been right about the man's boat. It was an outdated inflatable dinghy with a piece of wood for a paddle. The man jerked his rifle in the direction of the sea.

'Push it out.'

Peter pushed the boat into the water and jumped

119

in. For a moment, he hoped the dinghy would drift away, but the man was already dropping into it beside him.

'You row!' he ordered.

'Which way?'

The man jerked his head towards the tongue of the glacier. 'There.'

Peter paddled with his back to the bows of the boat. The German sat opposite him. For the first time Peter was able to get a good look at his face. The man's skin was like leather with large white scales flaking off it. He was smooth-shaven. A scar with thickened, jagged edges ran across his right cheek. It looked like an ulcer clinging to the skin. The man was almost a head shorter than Peter, but he had a powerful body. Peter felt sure he was in better shape than Andy or John.

He returned Peter's stare calmly. The glint of madness had left his eyes. 'What's your name?' he asked suddenly, in German.

'What?'

'Name,' said the man impatiently. 'Your name.'

'Peter,' said Peter. 'Peter Bush.'

'Hermann Karasek,' said the man.

Peter nodded.

'Hungry?' asked Hermann Karasek, putting his fingertips to his mouth.

Peter nodded again.

Hermann Karasek produced a crumpled packet from the breast pocket of his uniform and handed it to Peter. 'Here! Chocolate.'

Peter examined the crumpled waxed paper suspiciously.

'It's all right,' said Hermann Karasek.

Peter could see the brown chocolate through the

paper. His stomach cramped as if someone had kicked it. It was not just desire for the chocolate, it was a physical pain. Tearing the packet open, Peter stuffed the broken bits in his mouth.

'Here, not so fast,' said Hermann Karasek. 'Looks as if they don't feed you lot well enough. I've got more of that. A whole crate full. You only have to tell me where your ship is.'

Unable to understand all this in German, Peter shook his head uncomprehendingly.

'Ship!' repeated Hermann Karasek, angrily. 'Ship!'

Peter felt fear grip him, like an icy hand on the back of his neck. The mad gleam was back in Hermann Karasek's eyes. The same question as before. The man hadn't understood anything he said.

He mimed the movement of a ship on the waves, then dropped his hand vertically down, imitating the sound of a drowning man.

Hermann Karasek let out a roar of laughter. 'Wolfpack Frostbite!' he cried. 'Nothing gets past us. Torpedo, eh? Five hundred pounds of explosive – bang!'

The word *torpedo* is the same in English and German. Peter understood that all right.

'No torpedo,' he said slowly, emphasising every syllable. 'War over. No war. No war. Why can't you understand?'

Hermann Karasek's eyes narrowed to slits. 'Shut up, English boy,' he said. 'Nobody gets past Hermann.'

Peter shook his head in despair. It was pointless. Hermann Karasek just wouldn't understand him.

'Cheer up, boy,' added the German. 'We're not monsters. Come on, get a move on. I want to be away from here when your friends wake up.'

Peter paddled the inflatable dinghy around the

121

foot of the glacier. Hermann Karasek pointed to a rocky outcrop dividing the sea from the ice.

'See that cave? We land there.'

Climbing past Peter, Hermann Karasek stood in the bows of the inflatable dinghy waiting for it to touch the rock, then jumped out and made the boat fast with a short line.

Peter followed him.

'In here,' said Hermann Karasek.

'What?'

'The boat. Pull it up in here.'

Peter got the general drift of this. He pulled the inflatable dinghy up on the rocks and pushed it into the cave, which was big enough to take the boat and two or three men. He saw several wooden crates at the far end of the cave. They were grey, and bore faded white lettering. It said *Kriegsmarine*. The German wartime navy.

Hermann Karasek took the lead now. His rifle swung loose at his side. He walked very fast, and Peter had trouble keeping up with him.

They kept to the rocky ledge until it buried itself in another tongue of ice. Hermann Karasek climbed nimbly upwards. Only when Peter came closer did he notice the steps in the ice. After about fifty metres they led to a crevasse in the glacier. They followed the crevasse as it wound its way along, getting broader and broader, until Peter saw the other part of the island ahead of him.

It was farther above sea level than their own part, and four or five times bigger. The vegetation was the same: low-growing bushes and patches of grass. There were birds here, too, but nesting on rocky slopes higher up.

The far end of the island curved out into the sea

like a sickle. The southern side was just as rugged here, and there were steep cliffs with seals lying on their slopes.

Something large and rounded stood out against the rock in the sheltered bay formed by the curve of the sickle.

Peter narrowed his eyes. It was like a long cigar with its tip in the water. At its centre, he saw a stone wall with an iron tower rising above it. Even from a distance Peter could read the lettering on this tower. It said: U 98.

Realisation hit him like a blow. 'My God!' he exclaimed. 'A submarine!'

Hermann Karasek turned, grinning proudly. 'Surprised, eh? U 98, Wolfpack Frostbite. Karasek stands firm! Nobody gets past me!'

They went on in silence. After a while Peter was able to make out more details. The German U-boat would never take to the sea again. Part of the structure had buckled, and the iron plates of the hull had burst open to above the waterline. This was the stern of the submarine. Half the propeller was sticking out of the water, and a tangle of twisted pipes and bits of machinery could be seen among the iron struts of the hull.

The central section and bows of the U-boat were still intact. Hermann Karasek had built a protective stone wall in front of the conning-tower. There was tarpaulin stretched over it, forming a kind of shelter and entrance. Another wall had been built beside the foreship. As Peter passed it he noticed several torpedoes and ammunition crates stacked between the wall and the submarine's hull.

Peter followed Hermann Karasek behind the stone wall. At the spot where the ship had been damaged, the weight of the hull had torn an opening in the side. A man could get through it quite comfortably. Beyond it was a bulkhead with a steel door in it, still intact. Hermann Karasek opened this door and waited for Peter to go through it.

The light was dim inside the U-boat, and Peter stopped. His eyes had to get accustomed to the dark. They were in a large room containing numerous gauges, valves and indicator panels. Right in the middle was the opening leading up to the tower. All the light there was came from there.

It was surprisingly warm inside the vessel. Warmer than in the hut. Later, Peter discovered that the walls of the submarine had been extremely well insulated.

Countless sets of pipes ran along the walls and were connected to the instruments by pipe bends. Some of them ended in thin air. Peter suspected Hermann Karasek had removed instruments from them.

On one side of the room a narrow camp bed had been put up among the pipes, with five wooden crates side by side under it. This was where Hermann Karasek kept blankets and clothes.

Cans filled with fat were fastened to the pipes at several points. Hermann Karasek picked up an old-fashioned flint and steel and lit the wicks inside them. The room looked almost cosy by the light of these lamps.

'More chocolate?' asked Hermann Karasek.

Peter shook his head.

'Or I have meat if you like. Or sauerkraut. Canned, but it doesn't taste bad, and it keeps you from getting scurvy.'

'I want to go back to my friends,' said Peter, in English, but it was hopeless. Hermann Karasek couldn't understand a word he said.

124

He tried desperately to remember some more German. 'Friend,' he said at last, in that language. '*Freund. Good Friend. Gutes Freund.*'

Herman Karasek laughed out loud.

'All dead,' he said. 'First Klaus Metzer, then Paul Seidler. It was the loneliness that did it, you see, lad. Sit down on this crate. That's right. They'll soon be here. It won't be so bad, you know. You'll go to a camp. We treat our prisoners well. Only you must behave yourself, of course. You ought to be glad. It's all over for you. The war's over.'

Krieg fertig, he had said. Peter understood that all right and nodded vigorously, full of hope. Then he realised that Hermann Karasek had been talking about something quite different.

After a while Hermann Karasek opened a second bulkhead door. Before he went through it, he turned to Peter again.

'You won't run off,' he said, pointing to his rifle. 'You wouldn't get far here.'

He left the door open, and when Peter cautiously rose he saw the German's shadow moving beyond it.

Hermann Karasek was an unpredictable character. Peter waited until his shadow had disappeared. Then he ran to the bulkhead door leading outside. It was closed, secured with two metal bolts and a ratchet wheel. Peter couldn't get it open. Not yet. He would watch Hermann Karasek and find out how the mechanism worked. His chance would surely come.

Going to the other side of the room, he glanced cautiously through the open door. A narrow gangway lay ahead of him. It was almost dark, and several doors opened off it. He listened. Far within the submarine he heard faint noises.

His brain was working fast. They could survive

125

here. Karasek had. For thirty-five years, if his arithmetic was correct. Hermann Karasek had provisions and weapons and the inflatable dinghy. Somehow or other he must overpower him and fetch the others. But Karasek was dangerous. A madman. Perhaps that would give him his chance. If he watched him long enough, discovered his weaknesses . . . Peter did not follow this thought to its conclusion. His eyes were drawn to the red and yellow plastic housing of something. At first he did not recognise it; it was only the bright colours that attracted his attention. Then he jumped up and picked the thing up off the instrument console. The aerial had been pulled out, and when Peter flipped the switch the red light on the top began to blink.

Their emergency transmitter! No doubt about it. Someone had scratched the ship's name on the side. *Almax V*. The emergency transmitter that had disappeared with Bruce and the boat. Peter swung round. He heard footsteps in the gangway. He put the emergency transmitter back on the console. If only he could leave it on – but the red light would give him away at once. He picked up the transmitter again and tried to unscrew the glass cover over the light. He couldn't do it. The steps were coming closer. Peter struck the transmitter against one of the pipes, three or four times, until the light went out, then put it back on the console and returned to his crate.

12

'What makes you so sure?' asked Maurice Furnier. 'It's almost three weeks ago now.'

Julien Roussolet stared at the bows of the *Petite Mouette* for some time before answering.

'I'm not sure,' he said. He tapped his nose with his forefinger. 'It's just a feeling I have.'

Maurice Furnier laughed drily. 'We haven't found a single trace,' he pointed out.

'Yes, that's the point!' said Julien. 'Listen, Maurice. Fifty thousand tons of crude oil don't just sink to the bottom of the sea and leave no trace behind. If that tanker sank there *must* be traces. The oil slick should reach from here to the Antarctic. There's no way we could have missed seeing it. We've been sailing between fifty and fifty-three degrees for over two weeks. We've worked out the drift, the storm wind and the current. They just must be here. And even if we've missed them somebody or other would have noticed the oil slick by now. Did you speak to McMurdo Sound?'

'Two hours ago,' said Maurice. 'I've an idea I'm beginning to get on their nerves. They abandoned the search ten days ago. So far as they're concerned the *Almax Venturer* sank. It could have been a storm tide that simply ploughed them into the sea, Julien. I know

127

that doesn't often happen, but it's not impossible. Or can you explain why they aren't at least sending out distress calls on their emergency transmitter? McMurdo Sound has up to four flights coming in and going out daily. Someone would just have had to hear them.'

Julien nodded thoughtfully. Maurice had a point, of course, but all the same . . .

'Another week,' he said. 'We'll try farther south. Okay?'

'On one condition.'

'Which is?'

'After that we go straight to Rio.'

'Rio?'

'Rio de Janeiro.'

Julien laughed. 'Why Rio in particular?'

Maurice shrugged his shoulders. 'Don't know. I've had enough of the cold, and you and Albert and your stubbly chins. I fancy looking at a pretty girl for a change.'

Albert put his head round the wheelhouse door. 'Rio sounds good,' he said.

Julien nodded. 'Why not? The Atlantic's not a bad hunting ground in winter. Supposing we don't find the *Almax Venturer*,' he added. 'Because if we find her first, we can go straight ashore in Rio and retire.'

Maurice laughed, with a dismissive gesture. He put his headphones on and began listening in to the frequencies, one by one, for any sign of life. Julien looked at the time. Quarter to ten.

'Time for a coffee,' he said. 'Your turn to make it, Albert.'

Grumbling, Albert went to the small galley at the far end of the wheelhouse and put a kettle on the gas ring. Then he spooned instant coffee into mugs.

'We're running out of provisions, Julien,' he said.

'I know. This is our last chance, Albert. I mean it. This time the bank won't be satisfied with promises. They'll put the *Petite Mouette* up for sale. They've warned me they would often enough. That's why I don't want to go back, understand? It doesn't make any difference if we turn back now or in a week's time. If we don't have the *Almax Venturer* in tow we're finished anyway.'

'Well, I never reckoned to grow old on board the *Petite Mouette*,' remarked Albert. 'She's an ugly old tub.'

'Come on, don't say that!' said Julien. 'First impressions are deceptive. She has a heart of gold.'

'Quiet, you two!' called Maurice.

'What is it?'

'Ssh!'

Maurice switched the loudspeaker on so that they could hear too. The signals were coming through loud and clear. Short-short-short long-long-long short-short-short . . .

'The emergency transmitter!' cried Julien. 'We've got 'em!'

'Where are they?' asked Albert.

'Don't know,' said Maurice. 'I need a precise fix on our position, and then we want to take two or three bearings. I'd say somewhere within a radius of a hundred miles. An emergency transmitter doesn't carry much farther than that.'

Julien took the sextant out of the cupboard. 'Stop the engines, Albert. I'll get our exact position.'

'Right, skipper.'

Julien was laughing aloud.

'We've got them this time.'

13

Hermann Karasek put an opened can down on one
of the crates, and dumped a bent spoon beside it.

'Eat,' he said.

Peter caught the sour, vinegary smell of the sauerkraut. He shook his head.

'What have you done with Bruce?' he asked.

'Speak German,' Hermann Karasek said, in that
language.

'Friend.' Peter tried the German word he remembered again. '*Freund.*'

'Dead. Well, Paul was sick, you see. I'm not so
sure about Klaus. You know what I think? I think
he did himself in. That's my opinion. He didn't think
they'd ever come back. Ridiculous! And the fuss he
kicked up! He'd have been court-martialled anyway.
I didn't do anything to him, as God's my witness. I
tried to stop him, but he slipped. He drowned, see?
Right here in the bay. The water scarcely comes up
to my ankles, but he drowned there all the same. I
didn't push him down in it, really I didn't.'

Hermann Karasek's eyes were fixed on something
far away.

'You know what?' he said suddenly. 'You can teach
me English. I never liked school work much, see?

Hitler Youth and all that. Not that I'm complaining. Discipline, that's what they taught me. Klaus could have done with a bit of discipline. Only in those days it was all about the Führer and the Fatherland and the common cause. The hell with the common cause! It all comes down to people in the end. To what you promised. If Lieutenant Hartmann had told me to cut my guts out I'd have done it. I'll never forget the look he gave me. "You take over, Hermann," he said. "I'll be back in five weeks." That's the sort of fellow Hartmann is. A man and his promise, see? That's all that counts in the end.'

Peter looked at the floor. He had understood only a few words of this, but Hermann Karasek's eyes frightened him.

'Why don't you let me go?' he said gently. 'We'll leave you alone. I promise. We'll stay on our side of the island.'

'There, you see?' said Hermann Karasek. 'If you could speak a decent language we could have a nice talk now.' Suddenly he jumped up. 'Later,' he said. 'You stay here.' He looked intently at Peter. 'I want your word you won't run away. Your word of honour, or I'll have to tie you up.'

He looked expectantly at Peter, but as Peter couldn't understand him, he got no answer. He moved with incredible speed. Two or three paces and he was beside Peter, holding him tight.

'No tricks, English boy,' he said softly. 'Your friend thought he could run off too. Your word of honour, that's all I want.'

Peter was trembling all over, not just with fear but also because he couldn't understand what the man said, and there was nothing he could do about it. 'What are you after?' he asked quietly.

Hermann Karasek laughed scornfully. 'No back-bone!' he said, letting Peter go. 'No, you won't run away.'

It was a long time after Hermann Karasek had left before Peter could calm down.

He stood there motionless for some time, listening. Ten minutes passed, fifteen minutes, and then he plucked up all his courage and went cautiously over to the bulkhead door. Once again he listened, his ear pressed to the metal. All was still.

First he tried moving the iron ratchet wheel. It would twist only one way. He turned it four or five times, but nothing happened. Then he set to work on the two bolts. They would not move at all. But as he felt along the metal bars he found a small safety lever. He pressed it sideways, and the bolts snapped open.

The door swung wide, and Peter stepped cautiously out into the open air. He raised his head slowly above the protective wall. No sign of Hermann Karasek.

He looked back at the glacier. It would be five kilometres to the boat, he reckoned. Too far to go across the level ground, and he didn't know where Hermann Karasek was. He might be lying in hiding somewhere, on the watch for him. It was possible. Karasek was crazy, and he had plenty of time. Peter thought it over for a while, and then went back inside the submarine, without any firm plans in his mind.

The first thing he did was to pick up the emergency transmitter from the console and hold it to his ear. He couldn't hear anything. He wished he hadn't broken the indicator light. He put the transmitter back again and went to the second door. It was only latched, and the corridor beyond lay in darkness. Peter went back for one of the oil lamps. Its flame flickered wildly, but it gave enough light.

He opened all the doors. The radio operations room. The galley. The mess. The washroom. It was all painfully clean, and although the equipment, leads and cables had long ago stopped working and were now useless, they looked as if they had only just been fitted.

The next room was larger and almost empty. However, there were several long crates stacked along the walls. Grooves with rails in them were fitted to the floor, leading towards the bows of the submarine. Peter followed the rails. The walls slowly closed in towards the bows, and he had to bend low.

It was light in the next room along. The light came in through two torpedo shafts in the side walls. The rails ended in front of these shafts, which could be closed with a hydraulic seal. The room was half filled with grey wooden crates like those Peter had seen in the dinghy's hiding place. Some had been opened. They contained food: cans, and packets wrapped in oiled paper. The next room too, leading to the nose of the U-boat, was full of crates. Peter could not estimate how many there were, but he was sure they would last a single man his lifetime.

On the way back Peter took a closer look at the rest of the submarine. The vessel's arsenal had been emptied. He opened all the steel cupboards, but found no weapons.

He thought of the galley. A knife at least . . . although he didn't think he could ever really use it.

The galley was hardly bigger than a broom cup-board. Peter couldn't imagine how a ship's cook could have prepared meals for a whole crew here. He did find several knives, but he left them all where they were. He didn't fancy the idea of weapons; at the end of the day, he knew, it was your determination that counted.

A serving hatch linked the galley to the mess. Peter shone his lamp through it into the mess. The flame was too weak to light up the room . . . all the same, Peter saw a brief flash of something. He raised the lamp higher, and its light was reflected in a row of uniform buttons.

'My God!'

Peter almost dropped the lamp. A man was sitting in a chair scarcely three metres away from him. His head hung on one side, and his body was as limp as a lifesize doll. He was wearing a naval captain's cap and an army captain's uniform. The uniform was spotlessly clean and the buttons shone like new. Peter's hands trembled as he raised the flap of the hatch. He knew he was looking at a corpse.

The light fell on the swastika over the breast pocket, the stiff uniform collar. Then it reached the man's face.

It was a while before Peter could really take it in.

'Bruce!'

He felt something like shame. He had cursed Bruce too, like the others.

Peter held the lamp closer to the face, but it did not show him how Bruce had died. By accident, Peter touched the corpse, and flinched back, his lips quivering. He felt fear and fury and helplessness deep inside him. He could have screamed out loud. He didn't: he heard sounds coming from the other end of the U-boat. There was the rattling of metal, followed by Karasek's crazy screech. 'Where are you, damn you?'

Peter acted without thinking. He put out the flame of his lamp with two fingers, and then crouched down on the floor underneath the hatch.

Karasek's boots clattered over the steel plates of the floor. Peter held his breath. The footsteps went on towards the foreship.

'Come on out, damn you!'

The German's voice echoed loudly through the hull of the submarine. Threats, curses, an endless stream of them, and then he came back through the galley door, unhesitatingly, as if he knew just where he was going.

Peter pressed close to the wall. Hermann Karasek was opposite him now, hardly a pace away, separated from him only by the wall between the galley and the mess.

Peter dared not breathe. One more step and Hermann Karasek was bound to see him. But Karasek stayed in the galley. The heels of his boots clicked together.

'Captain Hartmann, sir, Corporal Karasek present and correct! Reporting an escaped POW. English. Unarmed.'

Karasek's voice sounded different. He had spoken with a short, sharp military bark, but that was not what really surprised Peter. It was a young man's voice.

'Yes, sir!' shouted Hermann Karasek. Then there was silence.

Peter's lungs were near bursting. He would have to breathe in. Speak, he thought, say something!

'It was a mistake,' said Hermann Karasek, and then again, louder, almost shouting. 'It was a mistake, that's right, Captain!'

'Stand at ease!'

135

Peter jumped. Though he could only half understand what Karasek was saying, he realised that this
was a different voice. Captain Hartmann's voice. But
it too came from Hermann Karasek.

'Cigarette?'

'Thank you, Captain,' said Karasek. Peter heard
him move, but he stayed the other side of the hatch.
The ignition of his lighter clicked. Karasek exhaled
with enjoyment as if he were smoking.

Peter remembered how Karasek had asked him
for cigarettes. He was sure the German wasn't really
smoking. It was all part of his game, like dressing
Bruce's corpse up in Hartmann's uniform and using
different voices.

The realisation came to Peter like a blow. He was
part of Karasek's fantasies too. Suddenly he was sure
of it. That was why Bruce had had to die. That was
why Karasek had shot at Len. He had simply written
off the future. In his world, time had stopped when
Hartmann left him promising to come back – the bit
about the promise was one of the things Peter had
understood from Karasek's ramblings. And that last
moment was all that mattered to him now. Like a
stylus going over and over the same scratch on a
record for ever, Hermann Karasek's life revolved
endlessly around that single point.

'Forget the English boy, Karasek!' said Hermann
Karasek in Captain Hartmann's voice. 'You've done
well, very well. We'll be off back home tomorrow. I'll
bet there's a crowd of girls who can hardly wait!'

Hermann Karasek laughed, embarrassed, a young
man's laugh again.

'There, Karasek, it wasn't so bad, was it? I never
broke a promise yet. You know why I picked you,
Karasek? I could tell what you were made of, you see.

136

Call it instinct if you like. I could rely on you to stand firm. You gave me your word, remember? You did quite right to get rid of young Metzer. Klaus Metzer, yes, that's the man I mean. Operation Frostbite was endangered. Your mission was endangered. Metzer had to go.'

'It was more or less an accident,' said Hermann Karasek.

'Oh, you're too modest, Karasek. Like that time with the bird-watchers. A pity you didn't get more of them. Watching birds while something like Operation Frostbite's under way! Still, two wasn't a bad score, Karasek. And no one noticed you, that's the main thing. They all thought it was an accident, that's why they finally gave up. Well, okay, old chap? Home tomorrow, Karasek. The end of Operation Frostbite!'

Hermann Karasek's heels clicked again.

'Dismiss, Corporal Karasek!'

Even when Hermann Karasek's footsteps had long since died away, Peter did not move from the spot.

'Karpog Island,' said Julien Roussolet, glancing at the nautical chart. 'Are you sure, Maurice?'

'A hundred per cent sure,' said Maurice Furnier. 'Is it inhabited?'

Julien Roussolet shook his head. 'Used to belong to the Dutch,' he said, 'but obviously the Australians made good their claim to it. Nothing there but glaciers and a frozen volcano in the middle. Doesn't look particularly inviting.'

'A hundred fathoms,' called Albert Malet, from the bows of the *Petite Mouette*. He was holding the coiled line of a sounding lead. 'Want me to go on?'

'Yes,' said Julien. 'I'll halve our speed.'

Albert Malet threw the sounding lead out in a wide arc in front of the bows of the *Petite Mouette*. As the line sank his fingers counted the knots running through his hand.

'Eighty,' he called after a while. 'Slow down, now!'

Julien slackened speed yet further. The land was two miles away at most. Maurice raised the binoculars to his eyes.

'That bay doesn't look bad,' he said. 'Hardly any surf. With a bit of luck we can come right in to the beach. What d'you think it is?' he added. 'A lifeboat, or just the transmitter?'

'Well, it certainly isn't the *Almax Venturer*,' said Maurice, scanning the length of the beach through his binoculars. Suddenly he stopped.

'Pinch me, will you, Julien?' he said, astonished. 'I must be dreaming.'

'What is it?'

'See for yourself. In the bay.'

Julien raised the binoculars. 'A beached ship?'

'Not a ship. A submarine!'

'Good God, you're right! It's not marked on the chart.'

Maurice laughed. 'Navies don't like to advertise their accidents,' he pointed out. 'They usually blow their wrecks up.'

'Wait a moment!' Julien interrupted. 'Can you read what it says on the conning-tower?'

'U 98,' replied Maurice. 'It's German.'

'That's right!' Julien laughed. 'Why, it must have been there for thirty years!'

'Ever since the Second World War, you mean?' asked Maurice.

'Yeah.'

They came slowly into the bay. 'No sign of the crew

138

of the Almax Venturer,' said Maurice, disappointed.

'But the distress signal's still coming through?'

'Loud and clear,' said Maurice. 'Perhaps the transmitter's been washed up by itself. They should have spotted us long ago. Give a hoot on the foghorn. It may just be that they're round the other side.'

Julien tugged the line hanging from the roof of the wheelhouse several times. When the last blast of the foghorn had died away, Albert suddenly took a tremendous leap into shelter behind the winch carrying the two lines.

'What's up, Albert?' called Julien.

Albert was swearing out loud. 'Someone's shooting at us!'

'You sure?'

'Of course I'm sure, dammit. The bullet nearly hit me!'

Before Julien could say anything else there was a loud report. A small round hole appeared in the wheelhouse windscreen, with fine cracks radiating out from it. The bullet had gone through the glass and hit the back wall of the wheelhouse, wiping half New Zealand off the nautical chart that hung there.

Julien and Maurice dropped to the floor.

'Now what?' asked Maurice.

Julien was turning the wheel with one hand. 'Let's get out of here!'

Sluggishly, the *Petite Mouette* turned. Then Julien pushed the lever of the throttle valve forward, and the stern of the tug sank low in the sea as the propellers braced themselves against the mass of water. Julien did not slacken speed until they were a good distance from the beach. Then he hove to, and they gathered on the foredeck.

'Did you see anything?'

Albert shook his head thoughtfully. 'I'm not sure. There was something moving on the beach as we veered away. To the right of the wrecked submarine. About the two o'clock position.'

They trained their binoculars on the spot.

'There!' shouted Maurice, after a few minutes. And then they all saw it.

'Good God – a German soldier!'

Peter jumped when he heard the report of the first shot. He had not been able to hear the *Petite Mouette*'s foghorn, but the shot sounded close.

Perhaps Hermann Karasek's hunting seals or birds, thought Peter, and if he's hunting he'll be too busy to keep an eye on me.

Cautiously, Peter pushed the door open. The light dazzled him. There was another report, to his left, and a flock of birds rose squawking into the air.

Taking precautions, Peter stepped out of the cover of the protective wall.

Hermann Karasek was lying behind some rocks. He had taken off the white snowsuit, and was wearing only his uniform. The rifle rested on a rock, its barrel aimed at the sea. Somewhere an engine roared. Peter had to stand on tiptoe to see the bay. His eyes fell on the *Petite Mouette*. For an instant, he felt as if he were standing at the lookout point again, seeing the mirage of a tug projected on the mountain. Then it went through him like an electric shock: this was real! Karasek had been shooting at the tug, and it was making away from the island at speed.

'No!' shouted Peter. 'No!' But his yell was drowned in the sound of the next shot.

Hermann Karasek sent two more bullets after the tug, but it was safely out of reach by now.

140

Then the noise of the engines died away, and the boat turned. Peter could make out three figures on the foredeck.

Hermann Karasek had jumped to his feet, and was doing something to his gun. Peter could hear him cursing. Its catch seemed to have jammed.

Slowly, Peter went towards the German. Suddenly he was not frightened anymore. He was blind and deaf to everything but Karasek. That was all that mattered – the German and the next step that would take Peter closer to him.

'Stop it!' said Peter. 'That boat will take us off! Don't you understand? We're saved.'

Hermann Karasek slowly raised his eyes. There was no comprehension in them, only the crazy gleam with which he had spoken of the past. And as he stared at Peter, his hands fingered the catch of the gun. It suddenly gave, and an empty cartridge flew out with a loud click. Without taking his eyes off Peter, Karasek pushed a new cartridge into the barrel and then charged it.

'We're going,' said Peter. '*Wir gehen.*' It was all the German he could think of.

Hermann Karasek's mouth stretched in a broad grin. 'Is that you, then, Captain Hartmann?'

'*Wir gehen,*' Peter repeated.

Hermann Karasek lowered his rifle. He straightened up and saluted.

'Enemy craft destroyed, sir,' he reported.

'Oh, do stop it!' cried Peter, desperately. But Karasek heard no one and nothing. He stood there rigid in his last salute, the salute he had given as he watched the other two submarines of Wolfpack Frostbite leave the bay thirty-five years ago. The wheel had come full circle.

Peter looked out at the bay. The *Petite Mouette* was approaching fast. She stopped just short of the beach. Two men jumped into the water and ran towards them.

Hermann Karasek did not struggle when Albert Malet gently took the gun from his hands.

'Come on, mate,' said Albert. 'The war's over.'

14

'What will happen to him?' asked Peter.

'I hope he gets put on trial,' said John fervently. 'He has Bruce on his conscience. That was murder.'

'He thought it was war,' Andy pointed out. 'When there's a war on it isn't murder. You get decorated for shooting people instead.'

'He should be in a mental hospital,' said Len. 'He keeps calling me Klaus. And Peter's Captain Hartmann, and he thinks the *Petite Mouette*'s a submarine. Can't get much crazier than that, can you?'

'We might not have been in a much better way ourselves after thirty-five years,' said Andy seriously. 'Can you imagine what he must have been through?'

Albert Malet came into the wheelhouse. 'You're looking better,' he said.

John raised a hand. 'Thanks for the clothes. And the shower. I feel a new man.'

'Don't mention it.'

Maurice turned away from his radio equipment for a moment. 'McMurdo Sound promised to pass the news on at once. Your families will know you're safe by now.'

'Thank goodness for that!' said John. 'I just hope my wife hasn't given my clothes away yet.'

143

Andy looked at him in surprise. 'You're married, John? Since when?'

'Oh, well,' said John, embarrassed. 'It's not that important, is it?'

'Not that important? Maybe I ought to remind you of a certain night in Sydney . . . not so long ago either, though it seems like forever. I reckon your wife'd be interested to hear how you and I and Sam . . . ' But here he suddenly stopped, and looked down.

No one said anything for a while.

'I wonder what happened to all the rest of them?' John asked at last.

'We didn't pick up any other distress calls,' said Julien Roussolet, standing at the wheel. 'Only the signals from your transmitter.'

'We were in the first lifeboat,' John told him. 'The sea was very high – it was chaos on board. We don't know if the others made it to the boats or not. Perhaps they never got off the *Almax Venturer*.'

'How exactly did it happen?' asked Julien. 'The fire was in the engine room, you said?'

'It started in the engine room. In the 'tweendecks, that is, but we wouldn't have abandoned ship because of that. One of the main tanks went up. When we launched our lifeboat the *Almax Venturer* was burning as far as her central section. All her systems had failed. Even the hoses were useless by the end.'

Julien nodded. 'What d'you think?' he asked. 'Did she sink?'

John stared at him in surprise. 'Well, of course she sank! Can you doubt it?'

'If I hadn't done a bit of doubting you lot would still be sitting on your island. The authorities gave up the search long ago.'

144

'Why did you keep on, then?' asked Andy.

Julien smiled, rather awkwardly. 'I want the *Almax Venturer*. Don't get me wrong,' he added hastily. 'I mean, of course I'm glad I was able to save you, but nobody's going to pay me for that. There's no law that says the people at Almax have to shell out for my expenses. So far as Almax is concerned you're sacked. When your ship sank or was abandoned you lost your jobs. If I could take the *Almax Venturer* in tow that'd be different. There are laws for that. Almax would have to pay through the nose.'

'I wouldn't grudge you the money,' said John, 'but I don't think there's any chance. You didn't see the fire.'

'No,' Julien admitted, 'but I've been on tugs for twenty-five years. I've seen more sinking ships than ships afloat. And a fifty-thousand-ton tanker doesn't sink without trace. Least of all if one of her main tanks is leaking.'

'The oil could have burned,' objected Len.

But Julien shook his head. 'No, that doesn't figure. Ten per cent at most burns. The rest floats.'

'Suppose the tanks stayed intact? Maybe the ship's lying at the bottom of the sea with her tanks still full.'

'Too much pressure. The tanks would bust.'

'There is a third possibility,' said John thoughtfully.

'And that is . . . ?'

'You're looking in the wrong place.'

Julien laughed. 'We've searched half the Indian Ocean.'

'Maybe it was the wrong half.'

'Impossible. We had your position – we had the latitude exactly and a rough notion of the longitude. And that fits in with what you've told us. You drifted roughly south-south-west for five days until you landed on Karpog. Since you didn't have any engine, the boat went with the wind and the waves, right? The *Almax Venturer* would have followed you. A lot more slowly, of course, but going the same way. I've compared the weather reports. After seven days the wind changed and blew straight from the pole. Another five days and the wind changed again, to west-south-west. It depends how high the seas were, but if they didn't change much after the storm the *Almax Venturer* should have been driven straight back to where she started from.'

'And you found no trace of her?'

'Not a thing. That's not impossible even if several tons of oil went into the sea. A fierce storm like that could have spread the oil over a wide area quite fast – and small oil slicks aren't unusual anywhere these days.'

'The anchors could have sent her off the course you've worked out, though,' said John thoughtfully.

'Anchors?'

'The bo'sun put the sea anchors out just before the explosion. We had to stop the engines because of the water being used to fight the fire. Bert Taylor – that was the bo'sun – he didn't survive it. I never much liked him, but he was right in the end. The sea anchors brought the *Almax Venturer* round before the wind.'

'Two anchors?'

'Two of them, with two cables apiece.'

'Two hundred fathoms – it's not all that much.'

'This was the first time we'd been on a deep sea voyage. Near the coast, two cables are plenty.'

Julien and Maurice looked at each other.

'It just could be,' Julien said finally. 'Here, you take the wheel. I want to look at the chart.'

He went over to the nautical chart on the back wall of the wheelhouse.

'The bottom,' he said. 'At a depth of two hundred fathoms. If those anchors held, the *Almax Venturer* should be bobbing happily around on the waves somewhere right now.'

'She'd have burned out long ago,' objected Len.

'But she didn't,' said Maurice, with certainty. 'There are a couple of flights over the area from McMurdo Sound daily. Even the most short-sighted pilot couldn't have overlooked a burning tanker.'

'The same goes for a tanker afloat.'

'Not if she happened to be off the aircraft's flight path.'

'Didn't they look?' asked Andy. 'You had our last position. McMurdo Sound could have worked out the drift too.'

'Maybe,' said Julien, shortly.

'Didn't you ask them?'

'No.'

'Surely you spoke to them?'

'Yeah.'

'What about?'

'Ah, it doesn't matter now,' said Julien. 'What are you getting at?'

'You know what I'm getting at,' said Andy. 'You never said a word to McMurdo Sound, did you? About our last position. You were the only vessel that picked up the distress call, and you kept our position to yourselves, am I right?'

'McMurdo Sound was looking for you,' said Julien, forcefully. 'Nobody asked our opinion. They obviously knew where to look.'

147

'We might have been home days ago if you'd told them,' said Andy, just as loud.

Julien turned away from the chart. 'McMurdo Sound did look in the right place,' he said. 'We wouldn't have stood by and said nothing if they'd decided to look in the wrong spot. And don't forget we were looking for you, too. Yes, I know, we want that tanker, but it comes to the same thing in the end. You think we'd just have sailed past you?'

'Yes, I do,' said Andy quietly. 'If you'd found the *Almax Venturer* before you found us. I'm not blaming you, Julien. I was only thinking of all the poor devils that didn't have our luck.'

'I'm still looking for survivors,' said Julien, seriously. 'I'll go on as long as I can. And not just to salve my conscience. I could be in trouble at sea myself tomorrow and need help, understand?'

Andy nodded. 'What was that you said about a depth of two hundred fathoms?' he asked.

Julien turned back to the chart. 'The sea's three to six thousand metres deep everywhere around here,' he said, running his finger along an invisible line. 'So the *Almax Venturer* could have drifted.' Then he paused. 'Here,' he said, tapping the chart with his finger. 'This is the spot. I'll bet you.'

The others clustered round the chart.

'The Ussberg Ridge,' said Julien.

Maurice leaned forward.

'It gives two depths,' he said. 'Two hundred fathoms and four hundred fathoms. It's a vast area, Julien. We don't have enough fuel to search it all.'

Julien nodded, his expression grave. 'Yeah, I know,' he said. 'We'll charter a plane from McMurdo Sound. It can do our searching for us.'

'Are you crazy, Julien? We can hardly pay our quay dues back in Cape Town.'

'We're playing our last card, Maurice,' said Julien. 'If we don't win this trick we're finally done for.'

Maurice laughed. 'Look at it that way and we can't lose,' he said. 'I mean, there's nothing to be got out of nothing.'

'It's best like that,' said Julien. 'Here, sit down with your radio gear and raise McMurdo Sound. I want that plane airborne as fast as possible, and I want direct radio contact with it. Insist on that. I don't want McMurdo Sound getting in ahead of me. Whoever sets foot on the *Almax Venturer* first has won.'

'Phew!' groaned Maurice, after an hour's hard bargaining over the ship's radio. 'They weren't what you'd call enthusiastic. Their planes are all busy. Everything'll be closed down in two months' time. They have to fly in all the supplies they can while the weather holds.'

'Did you get a plane, though?' asked Julien, impatiently.

'A Fokker Friendship. But only for two hours. They'll fly over the area on their way back to the States.'

'When?'

'Right now,' said Maurice. 'I'll switch the loud-speaker on so you can listen in.'

The Fokker Friendship came through shortly afterwards. 'Charlie Foxtrot Tango to *Petite Mouette*. Can you hear us, *Petite Mouette*?'

'Loud and clear, Charlie Foxtrot Tango. Come in.'

'We're over the search area now. Visibility good at five thousand. We'll fly over the area twice, on a north-south course with a fifty-mile interval, and then

149

we'll have to turn round. Sorry, but that's all we can do for you.'

'*Petite Mouette* to Charlie Foxtrot Tango. Understood. What does the sea look like?'

'Pack ice up to sixty-five degrees,' replied Charlie Foxtrot Tango. 'Fields of drift ice after that. The sea's closing up fast. Strong north-west drift.'

'Let's hope she's not caught in the ice,' said Julien.

'If she's there at all,' remarked Albert, but Julien waved his objection aside impatiently.

No one left the wheelhouse. Albert made coffee, and they drank it in near-silence.

Half an hour passed before the Fokker Friendship came in again.

'Charlie Foxtrot Tango to *Petite Mouette*. We have visual contact.'

The pilot's voice sounded almost bored. It took the men in the wheelhouse a while for the information to sink in.

'Are you there, *Petite Mouette*? We have visual contact with an unidentified vessel.'

'We hear you,' said Maurice, into the microphone. 'Is it the *Almax Venturer*?'

'We're flying lower now. It's a tanker for sure. Stationary.'

'The ice!' cried Julien excitedly. 'Ask him what it looks like.'

'*Petite Mouette* to Charlie Foxtrot Tango. Any ice near the ship?'

'Affirmative,' the answer came back. 'Vessel caught in an icefield. Drift ice. Roughly about four square kilometres.'

Julien swore out loud.

'Can you see any damage?' asked Maurice.

'Flying over her now.'

There was rustling and crackling from the microphone for a while. Then the pilot came in again.

'Extensive damage on the quarterdeck,' he said. 'The deck's burst open in front of the superstructure. Traces of fire.'

'Is it still burning?' Maurice interrupted.

'Negative. No sign of flames, no smoke.'

'How's she lying in the water?' Maurice asked.

'Normal position,' came the answer from Charlie Foxtrot Tango. 'Hull looks intact. We now have definite identification . . . lettering on the stern: *Almax Venturer*, Sydney.'

'Any sign of the crew?'

'Negative.'

'What's her position?'

'62° 41' south, 80° 25' east.'

'We're entering that in the logbook,' said Maurice. 'Positive identification as per charter agreement.'

'Understood, *Petite Mouette*,' confirmed Charlie Foxtrot Tango. 'You'll have to hurry if you want to get close enough. The drift ice is getting thicker the whole time. Best of luck. Over and out.'

'Thanks a lot, Charlie Foxtrot Tango. Over and out.'

'How long?' asked Maurice.

It did not take Julien long to work the answer out. 'Six hours,' he said. 'At top speed.'

'And I'll bet you're already on course,' said Maurice, laughing.

The sea was calm and the weather steadily improving as they made south, full speed ahead. Sometimes the sun broke through the clouds and its rays were reflected back a hundred times over as they fell on the ice floes. They were still able to avoid the drift ice. However, the distance between the icefields was getting less and less, and in the end they had to slacken speed. Only Julien and Maurice stayed in the wheelhouse. The others were standing on deck watching the ice. The floes were all drifting the same way. They were not very large, but Julien gave them a wide berth. The real dangers lay underwater.

'See anything?' Julien called from the wheelhouse.

Albert had climbed on its roof to search the horizon with binoculars. 'There – straight ahead!' he called triumphantly. 'About twenty miles. We've done it! She's ours.'

'Can we get right in to her?'

'No. We'll have to go over the ice.'

'On foot?'

'No other way. She's frozen right in.'

'Let me have a look for myself.'

'Can't be helped,' said Julien, a little later, clambering down from the roof. 'We won't get any closer than a couple of miles.'

'I'd walk a hundred miles for the *Almax Venturer*,' said Albert.

Julien laughed. 'That's not the problem. We can't get her out. Not until spring.'

'Then we'll just have to wait.'

'Not in the *Petite Mouette*,' said Julien. 'The ice would crush her like an eggshell.'

'I'm not turning back,' said Albert, firmly. 'If we don't nail her now someone else will.'

Julien nodded. 'We'll have to split up,' he said. 'But we need more men.'

'How many?' asked John.

Julien returned his glance unblinkingly. 'Four,' he said.

'On what terms?' asked John.

'One share per man in the salvage money. Two

152

shares to the *Petite Mouette*. It's a fair deal. I'll take you on at once. On contract.'

John made up his mind fast. 'Done.'

'Same here,' said Andy.

'Are you crazy?' cried Len. 'You're going back on board the *Almax Venturer*? For six months?'

'As a partner, Len,' said John. 'On your own ship.'

'Okay, then,' said Len. 'But I want to look at her first. How come she didn't get burnt out?'

'Maybe there was a tidal wave,' said Julien.

'It doesn't matter, anyway,' said Andy. 'The main thing is she's still afloat – dammit, I never should have doubted her.'

He suddenly stopped, and turned to Peter.

'How about you?' he asked. 'Are you staying?'

Peter looked at the hull of the *Almax Venturer*. She was completely encircled by ice. And she rode higher in the water than before. She had probably lost some of her cargo. Her superstructure towered up above the ice like a house built on firm foundations. And then he thought of Bruce and Sam, and all the others who had not survived. And he thought of Hermann Karasek, who had set out to destroy vessels thirty-five years ago. The sea wasn't a bad life, and ships were only machines. What happened to you depended on yourself in the end. On your own decisions.

'I'll stay,' he said.

Bob Shaw
Killer Planet £3.50

Remote, mysterious and deadly, Verdia is a world from which no one has *ever* returned.

But Jan Hazard is convinced his brother could still be alive and Petra knows Jan *can't* make it alone . . . on the Killer Planet.

Together they go in search for survivors – only to find themselves the next victims, trapped by the malign forces of a monstrous alien . . .

'A powerful story' SCHOOL LIBRARIAN

'One of the most impressive writers in the genre' SUNDAY TIMES

'One of Britain's finest living sf novelists'
TIMES EDUCATIONAL SUPPLEMENT

A. E. Cannon
The Shadow Brothers £3.50

The hearse was Henry's idea.

Henry Yazzie has lots of ideas. He's smart, good-looking – and a brilliant runner.

Marcus Jenkins practises being invisible. He looks like a giraffe, is lousy at English and kissing is his favourite non-contact sport.

The brothers love hanging round town in their first car – it's got lots of room in the back! Henry's lived with Marcus's family since he was seven but now they're sixteen and things are different . . .

Robert Westall
The Wind Eye £3.50

Monk's Heugh was miles from anywhere, up on the Northumbrian coast. Empty since Uncle Henry died, it was a weird choice for a family holiday. Predictably, the visit started with the usual rows. But when Madeleine stepped on St Cuthbert's tomb in Durham cathedral the children first began to feel the power of the old Saint's eyes. Following them. Watching them . . .

Cuddy had been dead for thirteen hundred years. What possible influence could he have in the present? And if he didn't control the awesome spirits of the Wind Eye – who else did?

'Versatile . . . talented . . . powerful . . . uncompromising' CHILDREN'S LITERATURE REVIEW

'A brilliant combination of the supernatural, family conflicts and the bleak setting of the north east coast.' VALERIE BIERMAN, THE SCOTSMAN

Rose Tremain
Journey to the Volcano £2.99

'Fear was racing in all their hearts, fear for everyone and everything they loved, fear for what seemed like the end of the world.'

George's world had been transformed. His sudden removal from his father and home in London to his mother's Sicilian family on the remote slopes of Mount Etna hurls him into a dangerous and wonderful summer: strange rituals, a sinister sense of the past and a vibrant vision of the present; then, an angry volcano threatens his whole existence . . .

Rose Tremain: 'She is among the most prolific and experienced of the twenty "Best of Young British Novelists" . . . and certainly one of the most gifted.' MAIL ON SUNDAY

All Pan Books are available at your local bookshop or newsagent, or can be ordered direct from the publisher. Indicate the number of copies required and fill in the form below.

Send to: Pan C. S. Dept
                   Macmillan Distribution Ltd
                   Houndmills Basingstoke RG21 2XS
or phone: 0256 29242, quoting title, author and Credit Card number.

Please enclose a remittance* to the value of the cover price plus £1.00 for the first book plus 50p per copy for each additional book ordered.

*Payment may be made in sterling by UK personal cheque, postal order, sterling draft or international money order, made payable to Pan Books Ltd.

Alternatively by Barclaycard/Access/Amex/Diners

Card No.   ☐☐☐☐☐☐☐☐☐☐☐☐☐☐☐☐☐☐☐

Expiry Date   ☐☐☐☐☐☐

_____
                          Signature

Applicable only in the UK and BFPO addresses.

While every effort is made to keep prices low, it is sometimes necessary to increase prices at short notice. Pan Books reserve the right to show on covers and charge new retail prices which may differ from those advertised in the text or elsewhere.

NAME AND ADDRESS IN BLOCK LETTERS PLEASE

....

Name _____

Address_____

_____

_____

_____

                                                3/87